Murder
at
Wimbledon

David J Staniford

Fulton Books
Meadville, PA

Published by Fulton Books 2021

Murder at Wimbledon is a work of fiction. The names, places, characters and incidents are based on the author's imagination or have been used fictitiously. Any resemblance to actual persons, living or dead, businesses, events or locales is entirely coincidental.

ISBN 978-1-63860-945-2 (paperback)
ISBN 978-1-63860-946-9 (digital)

Printed in the United States of America

ALSO BY THE AUTHOR:

Good Strokes For Senior Folks
The New You Publishing, 2020

Frozen In Time
The New You Publishing, 2020

Natural Tennis, 2nd Ed. With John Boaz
Stipes Publishing, 2010

Natural Movement for Children
Kendall-Hunt, 1982

Social and Emotional Development of Children
Canadian Association for HPERD, 1978

Acknowledgements

This is very much a personal story in the words and life of Jack Hardigan. As I have discovered, developing this work of fiction, pretty much from my own memory of these summers visiting London way back in the 1988 to 1995 time frame, you invariably discover that when you look at the past through a fresh lens, you see the world now differently. Just with the way women were treated thirty years ago has changed so much for the better, with far more opportunities. This story is unique to its time and reflects the values of that time.

The danger of writing a novel from memory of a particular time and location is that the task can be overwhelming. However, I did have a few relics of that time, some notes I had made at the time, also match programs and my tickets to the Players' Lounge and cafeteria, for example, triggered my thoughts to a previous time in my life. My thanks go to my wonderful editor, Sharon, for her unflinching devotion to the task at hand, in jogging my memory and pushing me beyond the limits of that memory. Her editing assistance of the proof and final manuscript was invaluable. To my daughter Lori, Jack Thompson, and my many friends, I thank you all.

To Dave,
Best wishes

David
Stanford

Introduction

MURDER AT WIMBLEDON is set in London in the early 90's. Jack Hardigan, Australian university student and tennis player spends several summers at the University of London and trying to qualify for Wimbledon. He tells his story of this time when London had several ruthless underworld factions fighting for the rights to smuggling of anything to bootleg liquor, cheap cigarettes, illegal gambling, extortion, prostitution and exploitation of young women. Set against a vivid background of Wimbledon with its class distinctions and traditions and with the threats from the Irish bombings almost every week.

Jack quickly makes new friends in all levels of London society. He takes us on his personal tour of London and the qualifying tournaments for Wimbledon. He meets sports entrepreneur and promoter Frank Brown at Frinton-on-Sea who leads him through a labyrinth of various characters from a lonely rich diamond heiress to several crime bosses. Sicilian nightclub owner Dom Gloriosos becomes a supporter and friend, taking he and Frank out on his luxury yacht on weekend cruises. He meets the beautiful, sexy Mirium during a weekend at her country estate. She watches him playing a tennis exhibition that weekend and finds she is in love with him. The story, as told by Jack in his own words comes to a disastrous sudden climax with a murder at Wimbledon.

Jack tells his story of that warm summer in London with great authenticity and empathy. He draws on all the grandeur and tradition of Wimbledon and tells of the great differences of class and stature of a society going through change. There is love, violence, sex and death in this story of a young man coming of age in a new world.

A Note from the Author

The character and voice of Murder at Wimbledon, Jack Hardigan is fictitious. I did attend Wimbledon from 1991–96 and spent time in London at the University of London. As a college coach I used my visits to recruit British players to play for me at Illinois State and Marquette Universities. My daughter did accompany me in 1991 and '92 and the story about Andre Agassi is true, as is the Michael Stich story at the Last 8 Club. I did play tennis exhibitions at several country estates while in England. Roger Ambrose, secretary of the All England Club, at the time, graciously hosted me several times and we played tennis on the back courts. I was privileged to visit the Last 8 Club, use the center court locker room, Player's Lounge, and sit in the Royal Box. For most of these summers I accompanied several groups of American high school tennis players and adult groups to Wimbledon with World Sports Exchange. I did coach several of my junior and college players in the qualifying tournaments and at Wimbledon. I did, also, play in a cricket match in the Village Green in Kensington—a highlight of my time there. Most notable of my time in London was meeting so many great people. These experiences and others gave me the authentic background and interest to write this book of fiction. I am hopeful that the reader will get a true appreciation of the culture and history of both London and Wimbledon and that they feel as if they are experiencing the events that unfold in this story. This is a slice of history, depicted in fictional prose. It outlines a summer in the life of a bright, gallant young man on his first whole summer London. This work of fiction will challenge what you believe about Wimbledon and take you into an era, before cellphones, social media and instant news to what is recent history. It is written today to reflect the attitudes and morals of the early nineties. As award winning novelist Erik Larson has said "history is a lively abode, full of surprises".

1

Wimbledon

It was 1991. Security was tight that year at Wimbledon. The IRA had made threats and there were a few terrible bombings in London with injuries and lives lost. Victoria Street Station was bombed putting fear into the tough Londoners. I was looking forward to another great couple of weeks at the big W, but with caution this year.

For two weeks every year in midsummer the top competitors in the world gather at the All England Tennis and Croquet Club to compete for the only titles which mean more than the prize money that goes with them. I felt privileged to be there as both competitor and spectator. I could not wait to see my name, Jack Hardigan in the draw for The Gentleman's Singles and on the match program. Wimbledon is not only a major world sporting event but also a major social event in Britain. Ever since A.W. Gore won the gentleman's singles in 1884, Wimbledon has been the event of the year, rivaling the Henley, the Steeple Chase, and Cricket at Lords. Being held continuously since 1884, except for the war years 1915-18 and 1940-45, when sheep grazed on the hallowed lawns, the tournament has been an event that has thrilled spectators, then radio audiences and more lately television audiences around the world. It has become an international spectacle.

I had gained entry to the series of qualifying tournaments through the Australian Lawn Tennis Association. I showed up at Frinton-on-Sea and got into the Singles and Doubles matches. When I went to London the first time in 1990, I was only there for a few weeks to take a research course at the University of London. This was late April, well before Wimbledon. That year the weather was just miserable, drizzly, cold and uncomfortable. During that week, I was busy and didn't think much about my tennis game, or Wimbledon. I did go out to the Queen's Club late one afternoon to practice on grass. That's where I learned about the qualifying tournament for Wimbledon. There was also something on about a qualifying tournament going on at Frinton-on-Sea. I decided then that I would get back to working on my tennis, get a letter sent from Australia and come back the next year and try to qualify.

Wimbledon at that time, was held the last week of June and the First week of July. Commonly referred to as the Wimbledon Fortnight. According to the British ITA, there was a series of qualifying tournaments held in succession before the fortnight. One could get a wildcard into Wimbledon by playing several of those qualifiers and doing well.

The grass courts at Wimbledon are the best in Britain, manicured perfectly for members only and for 'The Championships'. Center Court is not played on at all except during the tournament, except for one afternoon only, the week before official play begins, four ladies are invited to play doubles on Center Court to 'test out the surface'. This is one of the many traditions of Wimbledon. Just two examples of the magnitude of this event: Over 2600 Slazenger tennis balls are used and up to 24 tons of strawberries with 10,000 liters of cream are likely to be consumed, another tradition. As we went up to the main gate on Church Road, there was already a long line, even at 9.30am of those hoping to purchase grounds passes. Some had been there all night, getting their spot in the line the day before. The general rule of thumb is if you want to be in the Queue, as it is called, for Center Court and ground passes, you should arrive 24 hours ahead of the gates opening. This is not as bad as it sounds, as the comradery amongst those in line and with many of the players, who like to show their gratitude for your loyalty, makes the wait seem less tedious, and if you are really lucky, you'll be able to snap a photo with one of the players or snare an autograph.

This was the first day of Wimbledon, when the first round of the men's and women's' singles are held. It is not usually as crowded as the later rounds so it is normally easier to get in when the gates opened at 10.30am. Play on the outer courts started at 12 noon, center court at 2 pm. This was to allow the crowd to settle and for the grass courts to dry and be groomed ready for play. This was to be the day Agassi was to show up and play on the grass.

Andre Agassi had skipped playing at Wimbledon for four years saying he hated playing on grass and that 'grass was for cows'. He skipped any of the earlier grass warmup tournaments, such as Birmingham and Queens, for that reason. At least that's what he told the press. That first day I had several of my players scheduled to practice and play and I was eager to see them perform. I knew Agassi was on court 4.

I arranged to meet my two students Iris and Jane at the main gate at Wimbledon. After finding them among the queue I got them through security using my guest grounds passes. As we went in we were thoroughly searched—security was tight because of the Irish bombings threat. They were impressed. We had a good long day watching the outer courts and I got them into Center Court by arranging with one of my usher friends. They were able to take lots of photos and enjoyed having lunch in the player's lounge. They instantly took a liking to Andre Agassi with his long blonde locks and his denim shorts. I received a nice thank you note from both saying how they enjoyed the day, giving them a very special memory.

My story, however, started about six weeks before this. I had just arrived in London, planning on spending the summer. I was a student at the University of Oregon and was planning on taking some time to do coursework at the University of London during their second summer semester. Some of my mates from Australia and the US had told me how it was possible to play several events before Wimbledon that would give me a chance to qualify to get into the singles and doubles draws for Wimbledon. I could not miss that opportunity, so I planned my stay for the entire summer.

2

The Streets of London

I had arrived at Heathrow Airport after a very long and tiring series of flights from Eugene Oregon. The evening was warm, and I decided to go for a leisurely walk after dinner, to stretch out my cramped muscles, rather than unpack my bags. As I crossed into Hyde Park. I stopped to watch a group of young Brits and Africans playing at soccer in one of the grassy areas. When you truly enjoy playing a sport, you don't need formal fields and lines that you shouldn't cross. All these blokes needed was a plot of grass and a well-loved ball and enough light to see who they were running at. As I continued along my way, the dusk was giving way to night and the lights of London were coming up. I exited Hyde Park by way of Wellington Arch and headed up Piccadilly, preferring to stay on the main thoroughfares now that the night had closed in. By the time I got to Leicester Square, with its iconic Charlie Chaplin statue overlooking the fountain, I was getting tired of walking and feeling a bit lonely in the big city. Don't get me wrong, I loved being in London, it was unquestionably my favorite city. Coming from down under, the language was easy, although there were more dialects that were hard to understand and a lot more foreigners than my last time wandering the city streets, just a year ago. Was it just my imagination or had the city turned into the latest melting pot of the world? As a minimum it seemed as if all the taxi cabs had been taken over by Eastern Europeans.

It also seemed as if every political group was trying to make headlines, and the Prime minister's "Citizen Charter" aimed at giving power to the people, was being misinterpreted and twisted by many of London's criminal element, as well as political activists, as a call to literally and violently take back control of the streets. A very lame excuse, to be sure, but it had made the streets of London a bit less safe, especially for anyone who might be perceived as a favorite son of the government, or a 'hero' of the people, or for that matter, any celebrity. Basically, anyone with notoriety was fair game for assassination or kidnapping that could draw attention to someone's cause. It was difficult to identify who initiated half of this type of activity, since lesser-known groups would claim responsibility just to get their name in the papers and their moment of fame. One piece of correspondence from The Championship actually made note of this situation and encouraged players this year to be "cautious and alert when visiting our fine city's many attractions. Furthermore, it is highly recommended that you maintain a low profile and do nothing that would draw attention to yourself." Having always felt comfortable and safe walking the streets of London, by simply avoiding 'bad neighborhoods', I could not, personally, see where this kind of warning was called for.

I hailed a taxi and asked the driver to take me to the Kensington Palace Hotel. He was a warm, friendly and talkative Czech, engaging me in the usual pleasantries and small talk. He had been a dentist back home when his family made the decision to pull up roots for a more politically friendly environment. He was taking the required studies during the day to get his license to practice in England and driving a cab at night to put food on the table. His wife had the good fortune to land a job as a waitress at the Last Eight Club in Wimbledon. I politely gave a brief explanation of my stay in London, mentioning how tired I was, as a subtle hint that I really didn't feel like chatting. He took the hint and became quiet. I rolled down the window and felt the warm wind on my face. This turned out to be one of the hottest summers on record for London. For the first time in many weeks, I felt something of contentment, something like peace.

I had lots to look forward to that week, and I had my two British students to meet tomorrow and spend the day at Wimbledon with them. The following day my good friend, Joanne would meet me, catching the train into London from Nottingham to spend a few days with me. I was excited about my prep work for my studies at the University of London. They were going well and were very productive. I had some excellent material for my dissertation and would be able to meet my professors, mentors and other postdoctoral students in my own time frame by appointment. Last year I had struck up a close friendship with a chap named Frank Brown. I was looking forward to his companionship, and the social events that came with it, over the summer. He also had good contacts at Queen's Club so I could practice when I wanted to.

I had met Joanne the previous year. She was a beautiful, petite blonde with large, deep blue eyes that seemed to draw you into her very soul. She kept herself in great shape with well-toned muscle that rippled under soft curves. She was an art teacher and taught yoga part time. She enjoyed the diversity of her students. and liked to expand that sphere of acquaintances by taking classes herself. That is how she came to be in several of my classes at the University of London Summer Short Courses. We hit it off right away and we were involved before she told me she was married. She said she was unhappy in her marriage and took these summer courses to get away for a while. She said how much she enjoyed being with me and made it clear that she was not expecting, nor for that matter, interested in, a serious, long-tern relationship. We used this time together to the fullest, enjoying each other's company, without the overtones of regret or responsibility, quickly becoming inseparable for the remainder of the week. We had dinner together every night, went to the theater several times and to the British museum, and she stayed in my room the rest of the week. At week's end, we simply went our separate ways, though we had exchanged letters during the year and arranged to meet when I came back to London, this time for Wimbledon. I was looking forward to seeing her.

I had the taxi drop me off on Garaway Rd. so I could enjoy the short walk to the hotel. I warily watched as a figure walked past me heading away from the entrance to my hotel. He had his head down and a hoodie covering much of his face. I noticed what looked like a small white envelope tucked just inside of his jacket, as if placed there hastily to conceal it. After he passed me I turned and watched as he continued down the street. His posture and gate and attire were uncomfortably familiar. He had let the leather hoodie slip back a way, revealing part of his face. A streetlight illuminated him enough to catch a glimpse of a reflection in the windshield of an Audi parked along the street. Although the reflection was distorted by the curvature of the glass, it vaguely appeared to be the same man who I suspected was following me earlier in the day. I had seen him in my field of vision and his reflection in shop windows at Burberry's earlier in the day. He had the very dark skin of someone from the tropics and seemed vaguely familiar, but with very non-descript dark clothing and only discreet glances in his direction, I couldn't place him in my memory. Was he an acquaintance from my last trips to Wimbledon or was he simply a private investigator or someone from MPS or an underground crime network? Or was my imagination just running wild from the lack of sleep? The feeling of peace I had so relished earlier was replaced by an uneasy feeling that the future had just shifted to an unsettling timeline and I had a feeling somewhat like one gets when you sense a storm is brewing. I stopped at the hotel bar for a nightcap before heading up to my room.

I got off the lift and headed down the dimly lit hall towards the wing in which my room was located. As I rounded the corner, fumbling for my key, I didn't notice that the door to my room was ajar until I was about to use my key and I stopped dead in my tracks. Actually, that's not quite accurate, I stumbled backwards several steps. As I stood there deciding what to do, the bell captain happened around the corner and came up short behind me, almost knocking me down. He inquired if everything was all right and I silently shook my head in an exaggerated 'No' and pointed toward my door. He quietly moved between me and the door, gently pushing me back away while placing his finger over his parsed lips in a gesture of silence. He made two large raps on the door and immediately announced room service. We both held our breath and waited for a response. Nothing. He tried once more before very cautiously pushing the door open and announcing his presence with a loud "Hello?" With the door fully opened, it was apparent that someone had ransacked the room, as if looking for something. My luggage had been dumped onto the bed, the papers in my rucksack scattered all over them. It appeared the last thing to be checked was my shopping bags from the airport promenade shops, which I vaguely remembered had fallen between the mattress and the nightstand. All of the drawers, which I hadn't even used yet, were pulled out and tossed on the floor. Furniture was toppled over, and drapes ripped from the windows. Whatever the intruder was looking for had to have been very important to him, as it seemed at first glance that none of my belongings were missing.

An Inspector O'Neil showed up shortly after the hotel management placed the call regarding the incident. He had a forensics investigator with him to take photos, look for fingerprints, footprints, that sort of thing. They treat foreign travelers, particularly ones involved in high profile events, such as Wimbledon, with a bit higher protocol than the average break-in. Particularly with the recent political unrest. He asked me seemingly endless questions regarding all of my doings throughout the last two days, back to when I left my flat in Eugene, Oregon and anything before that which may have seemed suspicious. The questioning was exhausting and on top of a very long day and jet lag, to boot. He suspected that something had been slipped into my bag at the airport and the intruder was attempting to retrieve it. He indicated that it was an unnervingly common occurrence these days. "No one pays any attention to signs these days" he lamented. "Everywhere you go in the airport you are warned not to leave any bags unattended. Not even for a moment. Do people listen? No. Of course not. And then I get called out all hours of the day and night because some traveler has been burglarized. Only to find out that nothing is missing. Here's my card. If you find anything has been taken, let me know. We'll let you know if we get any leads." As he was walking out the door he added, "Keep an eye out, though, they may be watching you for a bit to be sure you didn't see whatever it was they wanted, and if they suspect you did, they may take action." and he closed the door. What did he mean, "they may take action"? I was beginning to wonder if this summer had any chance of being as enjoyable as I had anticipated.

3

Joanne

oanne arrived early on a Tuesday. I met her train, she looked
perky and beautiful, just as I remember her from a year earlier.
Her hair was that beautiful blonde color, eyes still that deep
blue, seeming exceedingly bright, and her cheeks a bit flushed—she
looked excited to see me.

We hugged and kissed passionately as though we had been away
for a year…and we had been. I took her back to my hotel suite,
which I had managed to get back in order before her arrival and
stowed her bag. She kissed me again and said how she was looking
forward to this getaway. In her letters she told me how she was having trouble with her school administrators. She told me all about
it and I listened. We then took a long walk, through Kensington
Gardens, and talked some more. We had a lot to catch up on. Right
away she explained how her husband had got even more abusive and
demanding, especially when he was drinking. She had moved out of
her house, and now had a lawyer who was wrapping up a divorce.
She was staying with a girlfriend who had a large country house.

We went to lunch at a small, intimate sandwich shop off Oxford
street. She unloaded all her thoughts. I listened. The therapy of this
helped her. She soon became more relaxed, took both my hands in
hers and kissed them, murmuring "thanks for listening and being
here". We got back to the hotel and learned there was a bombing

nearby. We decided to stay in our room. We watched the news on TV about the bombing, then took a nap and made love. She said she hadn't made love for a year. We enjoyed spoiling each other. We took a walk again in the park, sat arm in arm like young lovers. She was very happy to be with me. It had been a very difficult few months for her and she said I couldn't possibly understand how much she needed this reprieve.

It started to drizzle. It was a dark, damp afternoon. We decided to brighten up the day by taking tea at the Carlton Hotel. The Carlton was famous for its English Tea with its scones and cream, strawberries and clotted cream, and the cakes and sweets... Oh what a spread and served meticulously by their award-winning staff. We noted an equal number of male and female wait staff. This was unusual in England at this time as all the top formal restaurants had male waiters and chefs. We again had lots to talk about. We stuffed ourselves. The rain had stopped by then and we decided to walk back to my hotel. We walked by the famed Anglican Church at St. Martin-in-the-Field and then around Trafalgar Square. It was now quite mild out with few crowds and we enjoyed the walk together.

We talked about what to do the next two days. Joanne wanted to take me to the Cotswolds. The Cotswolds are in South Central England, comprising the Cotswold Hills and an area of many miles of green rolling hills and meadows. The towns and villages were famous for their houses and cottages built from the local honey colored stone. We looked at a map at reception and planned out how we could do this. The front desk could order us a rental car delivered in the morning.

We checked out of the hotel about 10am, after a hearty English breakfast and headed South in our rented Rover following our map. We made our way through Oxfordshire along some beautifully scenic routes. After about a hundred miles of driving we came to the Windrush River which flows through the center of the town of Bourton on Water. We walked around, had a late lunch and with the help of our waitress, found a quaint Inn in which to stay. We walked the town, enjoying the local shops and market. We rented some bicycles and cycled up along the river and down some lanes to some beautiful meadows and old farms. Everything was so green. We headed back to the Inn as twilight started setting in.

The next day we headed to the historic town of Burford, famous for its antique shops and afternoon teas. We spent a wonderful day there, took a long hike, then headed back to our inn in Bourton by the river. We found a superb restaurant with good local farm fresh cooking. We both ordered the leek soup. Joanne had the rabbit with prunes, and I had the local roast lamb. The fresh vegetables were superb, perfectly cooked and we shared the specialty dessert which happened to be Baklava. The owner was Greek, and he made it himself.

We headed back to London the next morning in time for her to catch the four o'clock train back home. This was more like how I expected my summer to start.

4

Jack Hardigan and Frank Brown

My passion for tennis began a long time ago. Growing up in Australia, I was one of those kids listening, glued to the radio in 1952. Every Boxing Day (Dec 26) for about the next ten years our gallant heroes were defending the Davis Cup on home courts. The city chosen for the matches changed by design, but we were always courtside by way of the radio broadcasts. Whether it was the fast grass of Memorial Drive in Adelaide or the slower ones at White City, Sydney or as a prelude to the Australian Open at Kooyong in Melbourne, we were there on the edge of our seats for every point. Over 27,000 people crammed into the White City Stadium on temporary wooden stands in 1956 when Hoad and Rosewall defended the cup-the record for the largest crowd at a tennis match, which stood for over fifty years. I was lucky enough to be a ball boy.

As my love for the game continued to grow, and through radio news and reading I became familiar with the tennis scene and its history, as it was played around the globe, particularly in London, where I dreamt someday to play at Wimbledon.

During this time my dad looked forward to this week for a much-needed rest from work. I was six and just started to get interested in tennis. My parents both played tennis on weekends and were always by the radio for Davis Cup. The great Australian tradition really started about then although we had had many great champions before that. However, the tradition as a national passion started, as it did for me, with these early radio broadcasts of the '50's. For those three days in January, the country stopped!

In those days, the holder of the Cup got to defend it. This was front page news, and not just on the sports pages—this was a big deal! From 1952 through 1960 we pretty much held the cup, defended it at home, hosting the challenge round. My first heroes were Frank Sedgeman and Ken McGregor, then of course the great Lew Hoad and Ken Rosewall at first as teenagers. McGregor, Mervyn Rose and Rex Hardwick helped carry the day in doubles. The stars of course were Sedgeman, Hoad and Rosewall in those early 50's with Harry Hopman as coach. No television then, only radio. I marveled how the two commentators called every stroke-especially in the doubles. When Hoad and Rosewall turned pro Hopman had Laver, Emerson and Anderson step up. Later, Ashley Cooper and Neale Frazer won Wimbledon and after Laver won his first Grand Slam in '62 and turned pro, Roy Emerson stayed amateur taking a lucrative contract with Phillip Morris. Hopman as well as Emerson, had other great young players ready such as Stolle, Mulligan and Hewitt and then as their turn came—Newcombe and Roche. This was Hopman's great Aussie dynasty!

I was unlucky to lose my dad when I was 13. He fought in the jungles of New Guinea, was a coast watcher in the signal corps. He died suddenly at 41 as a result of depravations he received because of having to live and spy behind Japanese lines. This sudden change shaped my life. I simply had to become more responsible for my mother, my sisters and myself.

I became a pretty good junior tennis player, qualifying for the Australian Open Juniors. I also played cricket and was a state league soccer player. I had a pretty good idea of the importance of good ethics from the great Australian tradition. I played tennis basically part time while working and attending University.

Early on in my freshman year, I was browsing in a used bookstore and came across a first edition about lawn tennis published in 1890. I was fascinated and read it cover to cover over several visits. It was priced at $100, which as a student I couldn't afford at the time, but it really piqued my interest in Wimbledon, its history, aura and traditions. It described the game, how it was played and the rules of lawn tennis at that time. It had pictures of the current and past Wimbledon champions, including the first men's champion, Spencer Gore from 1877. There were no Women playing until much later. I was captivated by this and started reading all I could find on Wimbledon. I was drawn in by stories of the Doherty brothers who dominated for five years before 1900 and Lottie Dodd who became the youngest champion before her 16th birthday, for several years in the 1890's. One of my heroes was Norman Brookes from Australia who won in 1907, not to return to defend until much later, playing in the final in 1914. Four time champion, handsome New Zealander Anthony Wilding, who tragically was killed in WWI, as an officer, fighting for Britain. I was inspired also by Suzanne Lenglen who attracted huge crowds to the old Worple Road site, appeared in the1920's, forcing a move to the present Church Road site to accommodate the huge numbers of spectators.

Before 1900 the game had spread to every civilized country, many Wimbledon competitors travelled great distances, practicing on board ship en route to London like Norman Brookes and Frank Hadow, who won in 1878, a big game hunter and tea planter from Ceylon. These internationals added popularity and prestige to the championships.

The early days of Wimbledon paralleled the growth of the British Empire. The dominions all were playing tennis, including most of Europe and the United States. In the early years of Wimbledon, the service was delivered underarm with heavy cut and groundstrokes were very wristy as with Royal Tennis of Henry VIII's era. Spencer Gore came to the net, which set him apart from the field. The net was the same as Royal Tennis, higher at the posts. Both Gore and Hadow, champions of 1878 and 1879 also played rackets and cricket for Harrow. William Renshaw dominated Wimbledon winning seven times between 1881 and 1889. He transformed lawn tennis from a polite pastime to a serious sport. Large crowds came to watch the wealthy Renshaw twins from nearby Cheltenham. Special trains would now stop beside the grounds during the championships to disgorge the enthusiastic crowds. Crowds from all classes of the era came to the grounds to cheer on their heroes.

The net was lowered at the sides and the service box changed to improve play with separate posts and lines for singles and doubles play. Playing doubles together, William and his twin Earnest created a new athletic game that enthralled the large crowds. They perfected the smash, the hard serve over the lower net, and aggressive volleying. At the time when William won first in 1881, he played only one match, the challenge round, the next year. There was a large entry the next year, in what was called the 'all comers playoff'-the winner to play off for the title against the previous year's champion. Once William won in1881 he played only one match each year, the challenge round, to win it in '82, '83, '84, '85. He returned in '89, much to the delight of overflowing daily crowds to win again through the all-comer's event!

After the turn of the century, the Doherty brothers dominated. Laurie was a sensation winning five successive years, with smooth, clean, and consistent groundstrokes. With his brother, Reggie, the Doherty brothers were invincible in doubles and the darlings of the crowd because of their inspired, skillful play and their outstanding sportsmanship. They elevated doubles to a main Wimbledon event. They were esteemed so much that when the Championships moved later to Church Road. The main gate was dedicated in their name.

As the modern game spread around the world, the net, courts, and ball were standardized to what we have now. A new motorized roller was installed, to replace the one pulled by a draft horse. This made the courts much faster, firmer and the overall surface flatter. Arthur Gore (no relation to Spencer Gore) at 41 years old became the oldest champion in 1909. Of particular interest to me was Norman Brookes, from Australia and Anthony Wilding from New Zealand. Wilding, a Cambridge student, the ultimate amateur, became the idol of the burgeoning crowds at the old Worple Road site. Winning in 1910, '11, '12, '13, he played side by side with Brookes at Wimbledon and Davis Cup for Australia. Wilding was an expert aviator and motorcyclist. In the winter months he rode his motorcycle around the French Riviera, practicing with royalty and the rich and famous. The world mourned when Wilding was struck by a shell in the trenches at Marne. Brookes became the father of Australian tennis and was later knighted by the King.

Deep down I wanted badly to be one of those young men paying homage to all those from the past years. It was also while I was at the University of Oregon, I got a taste for world travel and championship tennis at the highest level. The summer before beginning my Doctorate, I decided to spend some in London.

During an exhibition tournament at Frinton-on-Sea Lawn Tennis Club, I had met Frank Brown. I had just entered the bar after my match, and Frank, who appeared to have been sitting there waiting for me, waved a bottle of Beefeater in my direction. He frowned at the time. "It's five o'clock", time for a real drink. He moved to behind the bar, although he wasn't the barkeep, so I had to assume that he was a very regular patron. He poured out a healthy portion of gin over ice, added a bit of tonic and topped it off with wedge of lime. As a note of interest, Frinton had a prohibition against pubs within its borders, but bars were allowed at the tennis and golf clubs.

Handing me the drink, he began what sounded somewhat like a it might have been a frequent rant about the demise of a great nation. The look on the real barkeep's face, with the rolling of his eyes as he mouthed the words Frank was spewing forth, was a dead giveaway. "It all started in India. Those Brits were big gin drinkers in the hot sun—that was the start of the collapse of the empire. You Aussies were just too loyal, and, of course, drank too much beer in the heat. All that beer affected your heads and waistlines as well!"

After he came down from his soapbox, I guess he decided he had adequately, though far from eloquently, broken the ice and introduced himself. We spent the rest of the afternoon and good part of the evening continuing our way through that fateful bottle.

Frank and I both had a weakness for beautiful women, and there were plenty hanging around the tennis matches, the parties, and the crowds. This turned out to be a major distraction for me. I would be playing a match and find myself spying out a young one in the crowd, inviting her to tea, and bingo, only to end up listening to her life story. Frank was good for me, dealing with these encounters. As he outlined to me early in our friendship, he had these 'secrets to understanding women'. Frank was not the most handsome fellow, or extremely witty or bright, however the women really went for him. He had the uncanny ability to listen to them. No matter what they were saying or what gibberish they were espousing, he would listen. Invariably he would be rewarded. He became a great listener, and over time that summer, I did too.

I guess it really all started that year, at Frinton-on-Sea, when I met Frank. He owned a chain of sporting goods stores in and around London. As I represented Slazenger racquets, he wanted me to make a few personal appearances at his stores. We struck up a good friendship at the time and I agreed to make some appearances, do some book signings, and make recommendations on racquets and stringing for his customers. This was the beginning of what he called 'personalized professional service' for all his customers.

Frinton-on-Sea was one of the qualifying tournaments leading up to Wimbledon. I needed the grass court practice and play this year if I was to make a showing next year at Wimbledon. Frank agreed to sponsor me, providing lodging and a small stipend for the summer. I stayed at his large house for the duration of my stay, met his friends and attended their weekend parties. This was a real treat for me at the time. In return for the hospitality, I played some very informal exhibitions with the host's well-heeled guests. As a result, I became friends with many of these people, which meant that not only was I invited back, but had invitations to other country homes as well. Frinton was one of those towns on the channel, northeast of London where Londoners would go for holiday, for the few short weeks of summer to paddle in the cold channel waters and take in the sea air. They had a nice tennis club with about fifteen pretty good grass courts. A good place to get practice and match play before Wimbledon. There were about four or five of these pre-Wimbledon tournaments leading up to the first week of Wimbledon.

One other thing about Frank, he was adamant that a man should be smartly dressed, at all times, and for all occasions. He usually wore dark jeans and casual suede shoes, the kind that made no sound as he walked. His shirt was usually Fred Perry or a long-sleeved cotton poplin depending on the occasion. He rarely wore a business suit. He would wear a dark blazer for more formal surroundings such as the bar at the Dorchester or the 'Last Eight Club'. Jackets and ties were required for the Royal Box at Wimbledon. When we went for weekends at the various country home estates, we would all dress for dinner—a tuxedo was standard attire. All white tennis attire was required when playing or practicing at Wimbledon. He made certain on this trip, that I had all the proper attire to suit the occasions.

Frank and I had really hit it off from that first meeting. He was a tall friendly type, always able to take time to listen to people while at the same time taking care of the day to day demands of his businesses. He was one of those people who could seamlessly juggle business and pleasure. He had a lot of good friends and helped me get adjusted to London. He would show up regularly at my practices and matches. He appeared to me a straight shooter, honest and seemingly carefree at that time.

Shortly after meeting up with Frank on this trip, on one of my free weekends, he took me to one of his friend's country homes. As it turned out it was not just a house but a sprawling estate about two hours north of London. The sixty-room house was set amidst extensive gardens of prize roses, lush greenery, Romanesque statuary, and beds of flowers everywhere, the lavender and lily of the valley adding a heady scent to the air. The landscape was completed, in my eyes, with two perfectly groomed grass tennis courts and the ever-present impeccably manicured croquet course. Servants and gardeners were everywhere, discreetly tending to the maintenance of the grounds and every need of the guests.

These weekends at country houses have been a tradition for many years in England. Most of these weekends included fantastic drinking and eating parties, sometimes with a hunt, and of course tennis on the house grass courts. In most cases there would be food, drinking, music and entertainment on Saturday evenings. Several of

Frank's friends and business associates owned restaurants and night-clubs and there was always lots of actresses, models and showgirls in attendance.

I enjoyed myself immensely during these visits, but there was always a nagging bad feeling I had about some of these people. When I did ask my friend Frank about these people he finally opened up and told me the whole story. Many of the guests on these weekend visits were part of London's seedy underground. They weren't into drugs, but mostly into prostitution, cut rate alcohol and tobacco. A big part of their business was smuggling—anything from cigarettes to televisions. It was big business. They raked in a lot of money doing this which supplemented their legitimate businesses.

It was during one of the house parties that I overheard some things, I wasn't supposed to hear. We were at an estate in Withim. We entered through the gate and drove up the Hawthorne tree lined drive, which we had the good fortune to see in bloom. The drive circled around a fountain overlooked by a classic Georgian two-story brick mansion with Victorian additions on both sides. A valet, who looked more like a bodyguard than a valet, took our car as we entered through the double doors. The foyer gave a sense of how large the home was, with its two-story ceiling and the massive spiral staircase leading to the upper floor. The bannister on the staircase had been updated to more modern lines somewhere in the house's history, making it appear a bit softer and the foyer a bit larger. The furnishings reflected the current owner's preference of cleaner lines and less clutter than many of the homes we had been guests at. The artwork on the walls tended towards the look of Van Gogh's surrealistic style, which, for some reason, I always found a little disconcerting. I was more grounded in the classical style. We could see room after room as we were escorted by another very robust male to the back of the house, where most of the guests were on the patio, enjoying the late afternoon breeze. The back opened to manicured hedges lining gardens around a central fountain. From the elevated vantage point at the top of the steps leading to the patio, I noticed two men in the garden who appeared to be having a very heated discussion. They were partially hidden by the leaves on a low growing ornamental tree, but their emotions pierced through the dappled view clearly enough. Was it my imagination, or was the taller one the same man who had been following me?

As the sun went down and the lights came on, the scene took on an 'enchanted evening' appeal. The atmosphere and free flowing alcohol made the concern regarding the tall gentleman slip from my mind. I was, as usual, taking full advantage of the romantic setting to enjoy the company of the myriad of beautiful women at this gathering. The body hugging, semi-sheer fabric of their gowns left little to the imagination. I thought I noticed something like nervousness in some of them, but I was so distracted by their dazzling appearances that I dismissed any misgivings about their demeanor, or any possible reasons for it. I was too busy wondering if I could entice one of them to take a swim in the indoor pool after the other guests had left.

I needed to make a call to London to set up practice for the next week. I had noticed a phone on the hall table near the front entrance. Just to the left of a door leading into a study. The door was slightly ajar and as I picked up the handset, I noticed someone at the desk in the study was already using the phone. His back was to me, but I recognized the tuxedo as one worn by a seemingly soft spoken and congenial club owner I had met earlier in the evening. Even with the phone only partway to my ear, I could hear his still soft voice speaking in a tone that was anything but friendly. I couldn't help myself. I put the receiver up to my ear while covering the mouthpiece. I kept in a position where I could see if he turned toward the door or showed any signs that he was aware of my presence. A servant came around the corner and I hung up immediately, saying that it seemed as if someone was already using that line, and asking if there was another phone that I could use to place a call to London. I had hoped that I had depressed the handset button softly enough to prevent the parties on the phone from hearing the click as I hung up. The servant suggested the phone in on the table near the dog room just before turning left into the kitchen. As I walked around the corner toward the kitchen area, I could just see the club owner out of the corner of my eye as he exited the study. His steps hesitated momentarily on the tile floor, and I heard him briefly speaking with the servant. The servant continued on his way, and I waited for the club owner to start walking again. It was as if he was deciding whether to follow me. I heard the clicking of his shoes as he headed across the foyer toward the guests who had congregated in the dining room. I realized I had been holding my breath and began to breathe again. Had he heard me on the phone? There was no way to tell. He didn't appear to pay any special attention to me as the evening went on. There could be serious repercussions based on what I heard, if he even suspected that someone had overheard any part of the conversation. If he remembered me and thought I might have been listening to the call a little longer than I should have been, I could fully expect my wonderful summer to end suddenly and painfully. The call was about smuggling women from Europe for sale at the 'next auction'. Was this the reason for the unusual population of rare beauties and enforcer type 'servants', at this particular gathering? Were these women here against their will?

I thus became slowly involved with London's underworld. To top it off, it turned out that my newfound friend, Frank, had borrowed money from some of them. He had used the money to add more stores and to build up good credit. Unfortunately, these men would want to collect sometime, soon, with interest. Somehow, I didn't think they were the types who would listen to "I just need one more month" and reply "Sure, no problem".

5

Winston Gardens

Back in London on Monday, it was chilly with a steady drizzle. The events of the weekend were a mere blur. I had to cancel my lesson on the grass today and decided to head to the University to get some research done. A London bus churned by me as I came to an intersection at Oxford street. I turned slightly to read the ad on the side of the bus and in my peripheral vision I notice that the same man, who had followed me before, this time in a black leather jacket was following me again. Much too warm attire for the heat we were experiencing. Was this something to do with what I had heard on the phone line? Should I talk to the police? or Frank? I'd rather stay off the police radar. I didn't like the questions from the inspector. He seemed to be hinting that he didn't trust me. That night I had the opportunity to confide in Frank. I told him about what I had overheard and that I was being followed. He made a quick call, promising to introduce me to an employee of his. His employee named Nigel showed up at our front door about a half hour later. Turns out Nigel was Frank's head of security. Nigel was tall, rugged looking with very dark blue eyes that radiated competence and intelligence. His stubborn set jaw revealed to me that he may be dangerous when crossed. His simple grey business suit betrayed nothing of what lay beneath. After some discussion, he gave me a Beretta, showed me how to slip it into the waistband of my trousers at the lower spine of my back. He said "just for self-protection if needed or to threaten someone…dead bodies have a habit of spoiling one's trip".

The next day Frank took me out to the range at his club. Nigel was already there and showed me the basics of loading, firing and how to be accurate at short range. I had never been around guns before, but I learned quickly. Frank brought several weapons with him and we practiced for about two hours. The control and accuracy that I had on the tennis court seemed to carry over onto the shooting range. I felt confident with the gun in my hand, I just hoped I would never have to use it. Nigel couldn't emphasize enough or too many times—a gun was a last resort, and don't aim it if you're not ready to use it.

Frank returned me to my hotel with the rest of the day to do as I pleased. My room, courtesy of Frank and Slazenger, was more of a suite with a nice sitting area overlooking the gardens and park. It had a large queen bed, spacious bathroom and even a small shelf of books to read. It was perfect for my time in London. Frank was great at how he could arrange these types of things and a good friend as well. I spent the remainder of the day organizing my schedule for the next few weeks. I was well rested and ready for Frank to pick me up for our first two store appearances and a visit to a country house on the weekend. Frank said I had the suite for as long as I wanted. It was perfect. I could go for long walks or take a run up to Hyde Park through the gardens and enjoy the unusually warm sunshine.

This weekend we were heading out to Winston Gardens in Surrey. A large Tudor Manor with tiny leaded windows set back from the main road. It had a large barn with horses, greenhouses for fresh herbs and vegetables, a large, stocked pond that hadn't been fished for ten years. beautiful exotic gardens and three well-kept grass tennis courts.

We drove up the long stone paved driveway, protected by a forbidding iron and brick gate. The gate was open when we arrived—we figured they were expecting guests. We were greeted in the circular gravel driveway by the butler, George. As we unloaded our bags and rackets, we were greeted at the front door by the lady of the house who Frank knew as Mirium.

Mirium, according to Frank was "very rich and very lonely"— rattling around in the huge, old Tudor house for the past three years since her husband had passed. Their money was in breweries and South African diamonds. She spoke with a very slight Afrikaans accent. She disappeared back into the kitchen. After a minute or two she brought out a bottle of chilled Pinot Grigio and three glasses. She poured the first glass and handed it to me with an engaging smile. In the dim light this woman looked beautiful to me. It was as if aging had stood still as the years past. As I returned her smile, her lips parted with a quick inhale, as if suddenly and unexpectedly recognizing an interest in me. I had always shied away from developing my interest in older women, though I suspect she wasn't more than 10 years my senior, particularly widows and divorcees. They tended to want to talk too much, bordering on gibberish, mostly about themselves and their problems. The British women, in particular, just wanted to hear my Australian accent, as I expressed my empathy to their situations. However, Mirium appeared very genuine, worldly, and intelligent.

After lunch, Frank and I went straight to the courts to practice. Frank was a pretty good county player but was cannon fodder for me. I would usually spot him a few points a game to make it even. After a while Mirium came out to watch. She sat under a yellow shade umbrella and followed our play, clapping loudly after long points. I was flattered by the attention.

Around six, some of Mirium's other guests arrived which included two Saudi guests from the Saudi Arabia Consulate in London. Arriving later was our friend Dom Gloriosos and his latest shapely young girlfriend. We had drinks in the large reception room which had ceiling to floor floral curtains drawn back from the open windows, letting in a cool summer breeze.

After we had all gotten acquainted, we were ushered into the most elegant dining room I could have ever imagined, where the table was set for a sumptuous seven course meal.

It was still common for these parties to mimic the old, Edwardian style dinner party. As was customary in keeping with the formal atmosphere, the hostess had prearranged the seating location of guests, attempting to ensure a congenial mixture of conversation at the table. Whether by luck, or because she had hoped for some lively conversation with a younger, athletic male, Mirium had seated me next to her. She looked a little flushed as we sat down-her cheeks a little pink from an afternoon of sitting in the sun watching the tennis. She looked quite radiant from the afternoon fresh air and I thoroughly enjoyed the interest she showed in me during dinner. What I liked about her was she did very little talking, preferring to let her interesting guests guide the conversation. While most rules of etiquette were still followed, the modern day 'me culture' had certainly overwritten the prohibitions of discussing one's successes and status at this particular event. Dom talked about his second new club in London, much to the delight of his latest young girlfriend and about his new hundred-foot yacht he was now getting outfitted and hiring staff for a voyage to the Mediterranean. Frank bragged about his new exclusive deal with Slazenger and how he had signed me as their consultant and ambassador. He invited everyone, and any of their guests who wished to drive up from London to the exhibition the next day. The Saudis were very courteous and reserved, saying little, but smiling and nodding politely. When asked, Mirium said a little about the current diamond market, including the new, difficult to detect, diamond enhancements, while carefully avoiding commenting on more political topics surrounding conflict diamonds or the current trends in manmade diamonds. Diamonds as a topic seemed to interest Dom and the Saudis, as they made mention of the lavish necklace she was wearing.

The dinner was spectacular with fresh salad and vegetables from Mirium's garden, foie gras, fresh poached halibut, thinly sliced duck breast on a bed of baby arugula, and of course, very rare Chateau Briand courtesy of Mirium's French chef, whom she borrowed from her favorite local restaurant. Mirium leaned close to me to mention that the dessert they had planned was in my honor. To my delight and surprise, he had prepared individual portions of Pavlova, my favorite Australian indulgence. Named after the Russian ballerina during her tour of Australia and New Zealand, these meringue-based treats, are crispy on the outside, marshmallow soft on the inside, topped with a generous cap of fresh whipped cream and dotted with a variety of fresh berries. Dom announced that he wanted to borrow the chef for one of his cruises. We all retired to the outdoor terrace for coffee, brandy and liqueurs, and to soak in the soft mild evening air. I did regale the guests with my story of the Australian bushranger Ned Kelly, as everyone seemed to be content and, in the mood, to sit back and listen to a good story. There was Latin music playing on the veranda, at a volume that carried to the terrace as a pleasant background for conversation. I noticed Mirium's hips slightly sway-ing to the music, as if she wished she were dancing. When a mambo beat came on, I decided to break the somewhat reserved mood of the gathering. Excusing myself from my conversation, I walked up behind her and leaning close to her ear, asked if she would like to join me on the veranda for a dance? Not only had I been forced to take dance lessons growing up, but I had the added benefit of the athleticism and flexibility of years of tennis. There was also the added experience on the dance floor from the frequent coaxing of attrac-tive, single women to my side at clubs that I frequented. I moved in front of her and extended my hand to her in total confidence. She hesitated only a moment, glancing about quickly as if assessing the group to see if anyone would consider this inappropriate behavior from their hostess. She looked back at me with a defiant look in her eyes that said, "I don't care what they think! I want to dance!" We practically ran up the few steps to the veranda so as not to miss a beat. I pulled her close to me, then spun her away as we began to meld with the music, her torso undulating to the beat, her feet effortlessly gliding over the floor as she swayed, turned, and dipped, sometimes at arm's length, sometime up against me, in provocative moves that captured my imagination in a whole new way. The music stopped with her face inches from mine, both of us breathless from the exertion. My arm around her waist held her for a brief moment as we caught our breath. As I released the tension in my hand, she backed away somewhat suddenly, as if embarrassed by her display of shear abandonment to the music and my grasp. She hastily thanked me for the dance and headed back down to mingle once again with her guests. For the rest of the evening, I couldn't keep myself from glancing in her direction, marveling at the complexity of this beautiful woman, occasionally catching her looking my way.

We all eventually said goodnight and Mirium ushered out her Saudi guests who had to return to London. Only Dom, his girlfriend, who was very drunk, Frank and I stayed the night. Dom asked us out for a day sail on his new yacht the next week.

I said goodnight to Mirium and thanked her for the wonderful party. She placed a soft, moist kiss on my lips, when we said good night, sending a sudden jolt through my body. I went up to my room, drank some Perrier, then sunk into the luxurious, large, four post bed. My head was on the pillow, my mind drifting off to thoughts of the evening—suddenly I caught a whiff of Mirium's perfume in the room.

She slowly and silently slipped in beside me, as if not sure if what she was doing would be met by a welcome approval, as if she hadn't been with a man for a long time. As she came close to me, her breasts touching my arm, she began breathing softly in my ear, her desire evident as her breathing became deeper and the occasional quick inhale. I lay quietly at first, thrown off guard by what seemed like a dream, then slowly, as if I were afraid that I would wake and find myself alone, I turned toward her, placing my arm around her waist and drawing her closer to me. We started slowly, just holding and touching, enjoying the feel of our warm bodies against each other. The first tentative kiss quickly turned to passion as our desire for each other spiraled out of control. We made love several times before exhaustion overtook us. Our desires awoke with us in the morning, and we continued the activity of the night before. When we finally managed to leave my room, we were served breakfast on the veranda. I'm not sure, but I think I saw a glimmer of approval on the faces of the staff, as if they were pleased to see their employer finally show some interest in life. I caught a late morning train back to London in time to prepare for an afternoon practice at the Queen's Club courts. This was to be a wonderful new relationship.

I called her the next morning. I had to meet with my professor later that morning and I had the lessons in the afternoon but was free tomorrow. We made plans to meet in London in the morning and then visit Hampton Court.

I met her train at Victoria Street Station. It was dirty, noisy and congested but she was pleased to see me. I decided to take her to Hampton Court for the day to enjoy the history there and the tranquility of the gardens.

Hampton Court is about a forty-minute ferry ride up the Thames from London, the most magical of all the Royal Palaces. Hampton Court is famed for its splendid architecture and colorful past residents, but also for its extensive gardens. Its most famous resident was Henry VIII who played Court Tennis daily on his now perfectly preserved, indoor tennis court.

Five hundred years of royal gardening history spread across sixty acres of unforgettable beauty, Hampton Court gardens have long delighted visitors. There is a scale model of the Privy Garden in the indoor exhibition as it was during William III's reign, which was the tranquil royal retreat. The gardens and the buildings are as much a display of power and class as a source of pleasure. Mirium was excited to show me the exotic botanical treasures and the Orangerie where we found newly discovered species from the America's, Australia, and Africa. We stood together under the two-hundred-year-old great vine and took pictures as tourists do. We ran through the amazing green maze as if children in a magical place.

Henry VIII lived at Hampton Court and regularly engaged in jousting, falconry, archery, bowling, and tennis. Anne Bolin was an excellent Archer, as were some of his other wives, that is, before he cut off their heads. Arbors and covered walkways made the gardens perfect for leisurely pursuits and for the king's privacy with his many women. We visited Henry's indoor tennis court in the palace. Henry in his time invented many of the rules, customs, and terminology of tennis which survive today. He is actually credited with inventing the word 'serve'. It seems that as he became increasingly obese, over three hundred pounds, he could not throw the ball up to start play. What he did is have a servant throw up the ball for him so he could start a point. Hence the term 'Serve'. We found the palace and gardens a great historical treasure and vowed to return.

We caught a ferry back down the river and a cab to the hotel. Our driver turned out to be the same chap I had my first night here. I got a raised eyebrow of approval in the rearview mirror as he took in the sight of the lovely lady by my side.

The lobby was the usual scene. A few senior citizen tourists, a table of Japanese businessmen, and a couple of ladies of the evening at the bar, staking their territory for early evening revelers. The lights were dimmed, talking was low and subdued as if everything said was a secret. As we entered it seemed every head turned towards me, but not to look at me, but to feast on Mirium, who looked like she had just stepped onto the Royal yacht.

I moved to the bar and ordered two Tanqueray and tonics from the surprisingly attentive, young bartender. Having the good sense to recognize a couple who were interested only in each other at that moment, he motioned to a quiet table in a corner where two customers were just getting up to leave. We made our way to the table. The men in the Japanese business group were captivated by Mirium with lingering glances as she sat down and smoothed out her black skirt. I suggested with a slight grin, "why don't you give them a good look?" and with a mischievous glint in her eyes, she adjusted her hem just a bit higher up her thigh. It was fun to see their expressions, and a new experience for me to be with a woman, who could present herself as the woman of high class that she was, but who wasn't shy about showing her more impish side under the right circumstances. We sat there sipping our drinks, oblivious to the others in the room. She was easy to be with and didn't chatter all the time, a quality that I found intriguing and refreshing. We started making plans as to what we might do after Wimbledon. She talked about her life before her husband had passed and their summers in St. Tropez.

The Kensington Palace Hotel is set on the edge of the historic Kensington Gardens. From the hotel it's an easy walk to the Royal Palace and from there through to Hyde Park. The Palace hosts visiting dignitaries and is the London residence of members of the Royal family. It has been a royal residence for three centuries and is open for small public tours. The Albert memorial, one of the most ornate in London, commemorates Prince Albert's death to typhoid in 1861.

Queen Victoria outlived him by many years and expanded the gardens in his honor.

We decided to walk past the palace via the pedestrian walk connecting through to Notting Hill Gate. It was a warm evening with lots of Londoners still outside from their afternoon of birdwatching, bicycling, sunbathing, and jogging. After our busy day, we were hoping for an Italian meal for our dinner. There are no 'classic' choices in the Notting Hill area. For reasons I couldn't guess, even excellent restaurants here tend to spring up, then fade into oblivion or move on to other locations, so our choices were somewhat hit or miss. We turned up Portobello Road. Had this been a Saturday afternoon, when the market was in progress, this would have been jam packed with street vendors, carts, tents, tables, and people. As the song says, "street where the riches of ages are stowed, anything and everything a chap can unload, is sold off the barrow in Portobello Road." Being a weeknight, however, there were few people in the street. I had gotten into the habit of carrying the Berretta that Nigel had given me. It was carefully tucked under my light jacket, making me feel comfortably safe being out at night with Mirium. After reviewing menus in several windows, we decided on a small restaurant with a pleasant atmosphere of subdued lighting, Mediterranean décor, Italian instrumental music at a level you could hold a conversation, not too crowded, but enough people to indicate that food was likely palatable. The choice was a good one. The hostess, as well as the waitstaff, were clearly first-generation Italian (or excellent actors). Their speech, mannerisms, warm smiles and engaging conversation gave the feel of sitting at dinner in a small coastal town in Southern Italy. Add to that the fresh ingredients in the food we ordered, and we totally forgot we were sitting in the midst of London. We sat for what seemed like hours, comfortably chatting about life and travel. I carefully inquired about Mirium's past history with the diamond industry, sensing a reluctance on her part to talk much about it, but curious as to why it was brought up by the guests at her party.

Mirium, it turns out, knew a lot about the diamond business. She usually kept silent, especially after her husband passed. She outlined for me how diamond wealth in South Africa had evolved over time. Cecil Rhodes had exploited the slave labor after 1870, leading to his monopoly of most diamonds mined in South Africa. The Dutch, with the De Beers company, took over and amassed a multimillion-dollar fortune at the abuse and expense of the locals. In 1902 Earnest Oppenheimer, who started as an independent diamond dealer, settled in Kimberly at the heart of the De Beer's empire. The 22-year-old seduced the locals with his financial savvy and persuasive speeches and was elected mayor of Kimberly. He took control of DeBeers and passed on his wealth to successive ancestors.

As the hazardous slave pit mines became less productive, the people, already exploited, became ready to use any alternative to make money. As they no longer had the big companies to help with their needs, the miners, many of them children, resorted to other tactics to eke out a living. Mirium's husband's father exploited this desire. The miners and their families started cultivating homing pigeons to ferry out the precious diamonds from the mines and gravel heaps with the diamonds deposited in small cloth bags attached to their legs. Many of the birds survived, some were shot down by poachers, developing a shady, off company, illegal trade. Mirium's husband's ancestors had capitalized on the high price of diamonds, turning this into a vast fortune by investing elsewhere.

Mirium talked with me at length as to how these miners were unmercifully exploited, but by the time her husband took over his fortune was made and he just methodically and legally juggled his Swiss bank holdings, a large estate called Winston Gardens, with substantial stocks and shares in Dutch and British securities. When I met her, she had several accountants and lawyers controlling and reinvesting her wealth. Her main interest with the money was summed up by her comment, "as long as I don't have to deal with all this money, I am happy". She had a substantial stash of uncut diamonds and jewelry in local banks if ever she needed extra cash for her various charities. She told me she had no regrets for what had happened in South Africa years ago. She could not control a past she was not part of. She simply preferred not to talk about what had occurred in her husband's family well before her time.

When most of the other patrons had finished their meals and left, the owner stopped by our table and joined our conversation, delighting us with descriptions of his hometown, Cosenza. His enthusiasm for the region was infectious enough so as to cause Mirium to begin planning a trip there for their Chocolate Festival in October. He had the waiter bring over a classic chianti and Dulci per Adulti, a plate of aged pecorino cheese drizzled with honey. It was quite late when we finally settled our bill and stepped out into the still warm air on a virtually deserted street. As we passed by a deeply recessed doorway, I noticed a figure move out of the shadows. Since knives in the back were the current favorite of muggers, I didn't hesitate a second, but spun around to face the potential assailant. He was caught off guard and sputtered something about my wallet, while brandishing his knife in the air. I could hear Mirium gasp behind me. I held my hands up to calm him and then assured him I was reaching for my wallet in my back pocket. I brought my hand forward, pointing the beretta at him, cocked my head and raised my eyebrows as if in apology for lying, and asked, "Would you like to continue this conversation?" His face went pale, and he turned and ran down the street. I turned back to Mirium and she let out the breath she was holding. Then, out of nervousness more than anything, we both began to laugh. We continued to Notting Hill Gate and hailed a taxi to return to the hotel.

The next day we went down to Stonehenge, Salisbury Cathedral, and the ancient Roman baths at Bath near Bristol on a guided tour which Mirium insisted we take. She was good for me, encouraging my love of art and history. As I glanced around, I noticed the same man was following us, at a distance.

While in London, we explored some of the sights. We both loved the British Museum with its Elgin Marbles and antiquities stolen from Egypt. We visited St Paul's and Westminster, had some great Indian food and fish and chips. We went to the theatre, got there just before curtain to get the good seats at discount. We saw The Tempest at the Lyceum. Mirium took me to an orphans School where she was a patron. What a wonderful day accompanying a beautiful, educated women who shared many of my tastes. We were both tired and happily content and went straight to bed.

6

The Russians

Besides Dom Gloriosos, who's little empire covered most of the north and west of London, what became known as the Russian connection, controlled the east. Many believed at this time that their many legitimate business interests were fronts for their illegal ones, including human trafficking, smuggling, protection and drug trafficking. Under crime boss Uri Grosegann, MI5 and Scotland yard believed this connection harbored several KGB operatives in Britain. With a system of bribery and intimidation the 'connection' operated pretty much at will.

When crimes were committed, these guys were always suspected by Scotland Yard. Many new East Block immigrants were smuggled into London in the early 90's, given legitimate jobs, false papers, and new lives. However, after a period of time, they were required to provide something in return for their lives. Frequently a 'simple job' that if they got caught would surely send them to prison, if they messed up could get them killed by the very people that had protected them and given them their new life.

Grigor had been given a 'simple job' to do. It was time. The open lawn between the road and the house had darkened as the moon was covered by thick dark clouds. This gave young Grigor his opportunity to slip into a side window of the country house. This caper would settle his debt to the organization. All he needed to do was retrieve some documents and leave, undetected. He stealthily moved through the darkness, using only the light from various electronics, and the occasional nightlights to find his way to the masters' study. He had seen the layout of the first floor earlier in the week when he had posed as an unemployed gardener looking for employment. They had turned him away quickly with a token £20 note and a dismissive hand wave. He acted appropriately submissive and grateful, not letting them get a truly good look at his face. It was now 2 am and nobody was supposed to be home.

Grigor, who fancied himself someone between The Rock and James Bond, believed in just seizing opportunities, and headed straight into the study, moving a bit more confidently than he perhaps should have. Believing no one to be in the house, he did not close the door behind him, or even listen for other sounds in the house. He could see well enough from the security lighting outdoors shining through the sheer curtains to make out the furnishings in the room. The large indoor plants in front of the window cast eerie shadows on the floor around the two leather armchairs and table situated facing an impressive wood desk. The wall behind the desk was the typical floor to ceiling bookshelves. There was a floor standing terrestrial globe across from the door with a large original painting of a seafaring vessel, flanked by a couple of sconces on the wall. Grigor had seen similar ones in the window of a shop he frequently walks past for as much as £18,000. The décor was very expensive, but minimalist, with the woodwork details making the room seem complete. He headed over to the desk. Back in Russia he had been a woodworker, building fine furniture for the aristocrats. Once this debt was paid, his dream was to open a small woodshop in the outskirts of London and do what he loved to do. He had been told that there was a secret drawer on the right side, something he was very familiar with. There should be a release mechanism a few inches in under the desk along the right side of the leg opening. He bent over and ran his fingers along the smooth wood finish. Had he not been familiar with the design, he would not have detected the recessed release, carefully blended in with the surrounding highly polished wood. What appeared to be decorative wood trim above the file drawers popped out to reveal the shallow drawer. He pulled it out further and revealed a single folder containing the documents he was told to retrieve. He switched on a small pen light to check the documents to see if they were genuine. They appeared to be exactly as they had been described to him. He took the papers, stuffed them into his right pocket, replaced the folder and closed the drawer. He was so pleased with himself that he hadn't noticed he had made noise as he moved past the desk chair and it hit the shelves behind it. As he rounded the corner of the desk, heading towards the door his blood ran cold as he heard a loud, "who's there?" from the foyer. The butler must have heard him from the servant's quarters. With no time to lose, he darted for the windows, released the latch, threw the window open and disappeared into the night. Just as he was climbing over the stone wall, he heard the dogs let loose in the yard. He continued to run for a bit to get to where there were some trees for cover. He knew the police would be there shortly.

He started down a pitted, narrow lane, an old unused cart path. He walked casually so as not to attract attention from the few houses set back from the road. He headed for the railway station to catch the first train to anywhere…just to get away. He knew he had been seen by the butler, but thought his identity was secure because of the darkness and the hood over his head.

Grigor felt good about his retrieval of the documents. He had the papers and looked forward to getting them to Mr. Grosegann. Hopefully, this would be it, his debt would be paid in full. He was expected to deliver the document to Mr. Grosegann first thing in the morning. He approached the outdoor table set for one at a small café on Oxford St., where Mr. G was having a light breakfast of danish and coffee. Grigor was excited and nervous. He had been told to be sure that he retrieved the document undetected, but he got away without being caught and he had the papers. He just wouldn't mention the butler. As he approached, he noticed a dark figure loitering across the street, in stark contrast to the bright morning daylight, seeming to be watching the exchange. When he got close to the table, he motioned to the figure as if to ask if Mr. G was aware of his presence. The response was a quick glance across the street and an "is OK. You got the papers?" He extended his hand for the document, knowing Grigor wouldn't dare to be there without them. Grigor stood in silence as the documents were inspected.

Mr. G looked up at Grigor with a scowl that made Grigor begin to sweat. "Any troubles?" to which Grigor responded with a nervous shake of the head. "No one saw you"? Grigor was getting more nervous. He couldn't be sure if Mr. G knew about the butler. He did have an extensive network of eyes and ears. He responded with "No.". Mr. G suddenly broke into a broad grin, put the papers down on the table, and extended his hand to Grigor for a gentleman's handshake on an agreement and said, "So, you are now all paid. Go, enjoy the rest of your life!" He went back to eating as if Grigor was not there. As Grigor turned to leave, Mr. G. made a small motion to the figure across the street. He began to walk in the direction Grigor had headed. Grigor turned to look one last time at Mr. G and noticed the figure moving towards him. He began to run.

7

The First Murder

Athunderclap awakened us in the early morning. Mirium rolled over and kissed me on the back of the neck. I stirred, and she responded by taking my hand, pulling me on top of her. I could feel her warm firm breasts pressed against me. I entered her and her body rose to mine. Mirium gasped and seemed surprised at how she felt herself release and surrender to me. Her orgasm seemed to wash over her trembling body in wave after wonderful wave. We held tight together and then she started to giggle, an impish, happy giggle.

It was still early. I looked out the window across Kensington Gardens through a misty drizzle. There would be no practice on the grass again today. Frank had called and said he might be able to get us an indoor practice court at Queen's Club in the late afternoon. Mirium had plenty of time before her evening train so after a leisurely room service breakfast we caught a cab to her favorite gallery to see some of the well-known impressionists. The Van Goghs, Manets, and Monets, amongst others, were our favorites.

It wasn't raining hard so Mirium decided to walk around the shops and do some browsing while I went to practice at Queen's Club.

As I rounded a corner onto Oxford Street, planning on hailing a cab, a man running in the opposite direction almost collided with me head on. He came so close I could smell his deodorant as he grabbed onto my shoulders and pushed me aside. As I struggled to keep my balance, I heard a loud crack. I spun around, still not quite steady on my feet and froze in place. Just a few yards away, the same man lay face down on the footpath, blood streaming from one eye as though someone had turned on a faucet inside his skull. The dark red fluid flowed quickly onto the sidewalk, soaking into his white starched collar and custom-tailored grey suit. People in the street were screaming and running away from the scene, afraid, I suppose that the shooter would continue picking off targets. I knew that this was not a random shooting since this guy was panicked and running away from someone when he almost ran me down. In that instant, I realized that he had pushed me away, not just to get me out of his path, but to get me out of the path of the bullet he had anticipated. He had, in actuality, used his last actions on this earth, to save my life.

The shot had been loud enough to attract the attention of police officers a block away, who sprinted through the frantic crowd. I was shaken from my stupor by one of the officers as he kept repeating, "Are you OK?" while shaking my upper arm. About then the first police car and an ambulance showed up and I was ushered over to sit on the back of the ambulance. A medic did a quick check and confirmed that I was unharmed. One of the officers came over, again I was asked, "Are you OK?" but this time it was a question regarding my emotional state. He voiced my realization that "You are very lucky! You easily could have been the one to take that bullet." I looked up at his face and saw the sincere concern of a cop who had seen his share of innocent bystanders caught in crossfire and the pain that those memories caused. As my eyes lowered in the direction of my hands in my lap, all I could manage was a slight nod and a "Yeah."

Once I had regained my composure and given my statement, I was asked if I could be given a lift somewhere. I told them I had been heading to the Queen's Club to meet someone for practice. Although it was located in a different borough, the officer said to hop in, he'd give me a ride.

Frank was waiting outside when he saw the police car pull up and me exit it. He stood there, quietly, with his head cocked and quizzical look on his face, as I walked up to him, and said "Don't ask".

We were late for our court time, so we quickly changed and headed on to the court. Hitting something was just the exercise I needed to relieve the tension, so I was all power and no plan. Poor Frank found himself trying to return shots that either had him running from one corner of the court to the other or running for his life trying not to get hit. After about a half hour of this, I announced "I need a drink!" We headed to the locker room in silence, changed and headed to the bar. I sat down and ordered two Tanqueray neats. Frank had the good sense of someone who knew when to talk and when to stay silent. He waited patiently as the barkeep poured our drinks. I lifted my glass in a toast and said, "To being alive.", just as Mirium entered the bar, looking like she had thoroughly enjoyed her afternoon browsing through shops and like she didn't have a care in the world. We had originally arranged to meet here after our practice time was over. She took one look at my face, glanced down at the glasses of straight gins before us, and ordered herself a gin and tonic. Frank relinquished his stool for Mirium, and moved another one away from the bar, between us. I relayed my harrowing experience, as they both listened in disbelief. Somewhere during the story my hands joined Mirium's and without me realizing it, much of the tension that had lingered after the tennis practice had melted away.

Frank excused himself after hearing the story and Mirium and I decided to take a walk around Kensington Palace Gardens. She enjoyed watching the different varieties of birds and the unusual plants and vegetation. I was feeling relaxed as we enjoyed each other's company, as if the events of the afternoon had never happened. We decided to take the river launch to Westminster and then headed to the Strand Hotel for tea. We didn't have much time left before she needed to catch her train. When we arrived back at my hotel we could tell by the darkening sky, a storm was brewing. We just made it back inside the lobby before the first heavy drops of rain began to hit the pavement.

We were joking and laughing as we entered. Our mood changed quickly as we noticed that O'Neill from Scotland Yard was waiting for me. Mirium squeezed my hand and went upstairs to my room. Apparently, the detectives had identified the victim on the street in the grey suit as one of the notorious Russian mafia. After I dealt with the detective's questions, I went upstairs... Mirium's face was ashen. She showed me the headline on the Telegraph newspaper: 'Gambler killed—detectives seeking information.' Apparently, the man who was killed, Grigor something, was one of the henchmen of the Russian crime boss, Uri Grosegann. He must have done something very wrong to warrant the shooting. Mirium was worried. She decided to stay the night and leave in the morning.

The sight of her next to me as I awoke, erased all of the unpleasant events of the day before from my memory. I got her to the station just in time for her train back to her home at Winston Gardens. She promised to come back next week and stay with me for my first Wimbledon matches. I retained my complimentary suite for the next week while I was in the singles and doubles. I would be busy with practice and lessons and I really needed to work a bit on my studies but looked forward to her return.

8

Dom Glorioso

He had a wide face, big dark eyes, a black goatee beard, big bushy eyebrows and a double chin. He was about thirty pounds overweight for his 5'10" frame but walked with surety and an air of self-confidence. He was a major supporter of Frank's businesses and usually showed up at these country estate weekends. He wore exquisitely tailored Saville Row or Burberry's suits, except when on his yacht when he wore a blue blazer with white dockers.

For companionship he preferred young women—very young women. At his club he would personally interview all the new women employees, whatever the job. His current girlfriend was barely twenty and looked much younger. He spoke Italian with Sicilian dialect and French. His English was limited, however most of his henchmen spoke Italian. He always travelled with two bodyguards, so when he went to an event, or Wimbledon he had his secretary arrange passes for his guards.

He got no regular exercise; his skin was rather puffy, and he had a large flabby belly. Despite his physical limitations, he was surprisingly light on his feet and liked to bathe in the warm ocean at his estates in St Barts and Jamaica. He had considerable investments in Jamaica including a brewery and a rum distillery. He would accompany his guards regularly to the shooting range to sharpen up his own skills. He had large holdings in Milan, where it's said he started building his fortune in protection rackets and prostitution. He inherited an old estate on Lake Garda, with extensive wine cellars, lemon and olive groves. He often boasted at parties that his lemons from the town of Limone, on the shores of Lake Garda, were the best in the world—and they were. Golden, large and succulent he would always take a box for the host of weekend parties he attended.

He always drank the best Italian wines with his favorites being the deep, complex Brunello's from the Umbra district of Northern Italy. He drank copious amounts of these wines with the Sicilian lamb he imported as a main feature at his restaurants in London. He spent liberally on his girlfriends, "to keep them happy", he would say. He spent the winters, usually on the French or Italian Riviera, commuting from Cannes by private jet once a week to London to take care of his private clubs and restaurants, or to trade in girlfriends.

Despite the many rumors of his underworld dealings in smuggling and prostitution he was always a jovial host and was good company for his guests. Dom's main opposition came from the Russian mafia in London. These guys were an extension of the richest Russian oligarchs and were reported to be ruthless if you crossed them. They pretty much controlled all the prostitution, smuggling and illegal gambling clubs in London's east end. Both the Poles and Russians were jealous of Dom's territory. My friend Frank really liked Dom and always spoke highly of him. It seemed that once Dom liked you and your company, he would endeavor to become a loyal friend. His yacht Ruby Belle was his newest acquisition. He liked his business associates, his women and his friends in the sports world, including football players, famous cricketers and now tennis players to come to his clubs or as guests on his new yacht.

It was still two weeks before Wimbledon. Dom had invited us for a day on his yacht. What a glorious day it was and what a yacht— all one hundred feet of it. It was one of those few warm and sunny days in London—the Thames never looked so good, now they had cleaned it up.

We were met precisely at 11am by Dom's skiff to take us out to his mooring. After a short ride we could see we were in for a treat. We were looking at one hundred feet of pure luxury. Our host greeted us in grand style, got champagne in our hands as we got under way and proudly gave us a tour of his new toy. We were aboard a sleek white motor yacht with all the trimmings, fully staffed with deck hands, two chefs, trained butlers. The aft deck was equipped with a fighting chair for the sport's fisherman, and also stored two Yamaha wave runners when underway. I also noticed a set of golf clubs tucked away in a corner in case you chose to tee up on the bow. On the sun deck there was a fully stocked wet bar, lounge chairs and cushions everywhere. This is also where we found a large hot tub, complete with Dom's favorite showgirls from his London clubs, giggling and waving as we walked through. The interior was entirely decked out with cherry walls and cabinetry, oriental rugs, luxury sofas and chairs, a glass top dining room table set for 8, recessed lighting everywhere and 4 staterooms. The fully equipped and applianced galley below deck was complete with black marble countertops with a breakfast bar and an adjoining elevated breakfast nook with an oval black marble table and cushioned bench seating on three sides. The bridge was uncluttered with all the necessary instrumentation and monitors required to operate a vessel this size. It also included as corner table with fully cushioned bench seating and a separate communication desk. The upper deck included a conference/gaming table with a beautiful inlaid compass rose at the center and more deeply cushioned seating along the aft wall. We did not bother going down to the engine room. We had seen quite enough!

I did not know any of the other guests on board, but they knew me. I was 'that Aussie tennis player'. I was pronounced famous by my friend Frank, courtesy of the article in the Daily Mirror. Frank was pleased as this helped create publicity for his stores and for the release, with great fanfare, of the new, made in England, Slazenger N01 racket and clothing line.

Dom was jubilant—introducing me all around and to all his showgirls. Pretty soon we were all in the hot tub with more drinks. This was going to be a great day! We cruised along the river, oblivious to the sights, other than those within a few feet of us. We soaked, we swam, we drank and we played cards, we ate. The chef's put out a delightful lunch of assorted panini sandwiches and Waldorf salad. Later they prepared a light supper of poached salmon with a dill sauce, sitting on a bed of baby spinach leaves and accompanied by side dish of sautéed aubergine, (known in the states as eggplant). Some mini cream puffs and coffee rounded out our day.

After a day in the fresh air, with copious amounts of alcohol, water sports and sun, I was feeling very content and tired as I got out of the cab at my hotel. I vaguely remember an exaggeratedly grandiose bow, complete with sweeping an imaginary hat through the air, in the direction of the young lady behind the counter as I bid her a good night and continued to stumble up to my room. Sleep overcame me before my head was even on the pillow. My dreams, however, were not so peaceful.

I was running through the streets near Wimbledon, with rain pelting down. As I turned a corner, the puddles turned to blood and the thunder sounded more like gun shots. As I ran into one puddle, it began to spin and I was suddenly being drawn into a whirlpool of what I can best describe as a swirling kaleidoscope of scenes from the Portobello Road market, where half of the people were wearing black leather jackets. As I continued to be drawn down, I was awakened by the crack of lightening in my dream. I lay there, in a cold sweat, heart racing, breathing heavily. Sleep overcame me quickly once again. This time without the dreams. I awoke in the morning and took a long shower, as the memories from the dream were slowly washed away.

Later that week I invited Dom to Wimbledon to take tea on the terrace overlooking the courts and then for drinks at the Last 8 Club on the Wimbledon grounds as a thank you for a great day. The Last 8 Club is an extremely exclusive club only open to Wimbledon Quarterfinalists. Dom of course was excited to be there, for while he had the resources to mingle with the upper crust in London, his association with the less desirable elements of British society kept him from being welcomed with open arms at certain of the more elite gathering spots in town. This was also the perfect opportunity to show off his latest, new girlfriend. In typical fashion, she excused herself to 'powder her nose'. Being the owner of several clubs does have its advantages when seeking beautiful female companionship. His visit here at the Last 8 Club had been arranged by Frank and I, through Slazenger, who supplies all the tennis balls for Wimbledon. This allows them to pull a few strings to bend the rules. My good friend, Roger Ambrose, Secretary of the All England Club joined us. Wimbledon Champion Michael Stich was also to join us. We were all sitting all seated at the very somewhat intimate, currently crowded by our presence, bar when Michael arrived with his fiancé, Brenda. He had pushed the door open and allowed her to enter the room first. When she entered the room, a sudden deep hush fell over the room as conversations were stopped mid-sentence, mouths still open with words dangling in midair. Dom turned to look, and his jaw dropped to the floor. Roger, who had been casually leaning over the bar, shot up out of his chair to stand in her presence, almost knocking over his drink. Frank turned and sat erect in his seat as he let out a long, low whistle. I just stood there, dumbstruck. All eyes at the tables scattered about followed her as she glided across the room, on long, shapely legs made even longer by the high heeled sandals that showed off every curve and accentuated the fluid movement of every muscle. Her hips were cradled in a mid-thigh pencil skirt with a slit over the left thigh that seemed to wink at you with each step she took. The curve of her hips seemed to melt into a perfectly proportioned waist. Her blouse was loosely tucked in her skirt, with no buttons above her midriff, but with a draped shawl collar that allowed only glimpses of flesh as she moved. Her long, slender neck emerged from the folds of the fabric as an elegant pedestal for what I can only describe as the most perfect face I have every laid my eyes on, framed by thick, shimmering, dark blonde hair, pulled up with a cascade of curls down her back. Her skin was flawless, with just a hint of color in the cheeks, her lips full and in a seemingly endless smile. Her large, emerald-green eyes seemed to dance with the reflection of every light in the room. She was unmistakably, gorgeous. You could have heard a pin drop! As she made her way to our little group, the conversation in the room quickly went back to normal, as if embarrassed by the abrupt pause. She carried herself with confidence, but at the same time, seemed oblivious to the attention that she drew. Dom, who was always surrounded by beautiful women, was clearly very impressed, and finally closed his mouth. Michael caught up to her and placed his hand lovingly on her waist. She leaned back in towards him and whispered something softly in his ear. I can't be sure with the dim lighting, but I do believe he was blushing.

She was a knockout! Dom moved over to allow her and Michael to sit together. Dom was used to being around dancers at his clubs, where the rules of engagement were clearly different than these circumstances. He seemed to be genuinely struggling not to reach out and touch her. His eyes nearly bugged out of his head as she wriggled onto the stool, showing off those long shapely legs. About that time, Dom's girlfriend arrived back on the scene, not having been privy to the reaction the new woman in the group had caused. She seemed to scowl a bit as she was introduced but managed to hold her own in conversation with her during the course of the evening. It was an evening to remember. We visited with Michael and his girl for about an hour. When they left, Dom sprang up, apparently forgetting the date at his side, and reached over to Michael's fiancée's stool and softly caressed the fine leather where she had been sitting, giving out a very long dramatic sigh. With the exception of the young woman with him, who simply rolled her eyes in disgust at this all too familiar male behavior, we all broke out into a raucous laugh. Dom was not going to live this down anytime soon. What a time we were having. Dom picked up the very substantial check.

9

The Second Murder

ecause Dom had such a good time at the Last Eight Club, we decided to invite him again. I went over to Wimbledon in one of the club's courtesy cars to get my scheduled practice in at 1pm. Wimbledon had a rule of no play or practice before noon. I hit with my friend Aaron Wasson, who had signed us up to play doubles in the main draw. We were not sure if we were in the draw yet, but we were finalists at Frinton and Edgbaston during qualifying and we were hopeful we would get to play the next week on the Wednesday or Thursday of the first week of Wimbledon.

We met Frank in the locker room after, where we enjoyed a luxurious soak in their huge individual tubs and a deep massage by their masseurs (masseuses were not allowed on the men's side at Wimbledon), who had many stories to tell us about Wimbledon over the years. We were able to order beers there from the bar in the locker rooms, to add to our feeling of total relaxation. We were feeling pretty good when we showered and went upstairs to the Last Eight Club, where we had arranged for Dom to meet us. Aaron joined us as he hadn't met Dom yet. Dom was a little peeved as his bodyguard was not allowed in the grounds with the heightened security. It hadn't occurred to us to include him in on the invitation.

We all stayed on till quite late, it had been a great day, topped off with a great dinner, followed by coffee and the requisite digestif.

We all exited the grounds at the Church Road gate in high spirits. Several bobbies were standing around on the parking lot side of the gate, as the last few of the members and staff left the grounds. As we moved past the security booth and out the Church St. gate, the area shook with the rumble of distant thunder. My gaze looked skyward, dark clouds were gathering. The first raindrops started to fall. There was another rumble of thunder, this one closer. We stood there on the curb waiting for Dom's limousine to come around, hoping we would be able to get into the limo before getting soaked. Suddenly, there were two muffled cracks. From my recent experience at the shooting range, I instantly identified the sound. Dom fell to the ground. The bobbies came running. The few other people in the area either scattered or hit the ground. I looked in the direction the sounds had come from, just in time to see the familiar form of the man in the black leather jacket dodge into the shadows behind several bushes on the golf course side of the fence. I yelled to the bobbies, but in the confusion, they did not immediately hear me. By the time I had gotten their full attention directed to where the shooter had been, he had a good 30 seconds to have disappeared. There had been some event at the Wimbledon Club across the street that had recently ended, so there was a steady stream of cars leaving the driveway a few yards from where the shooter had been Any one of them could have been the shooter. By the time the traffic was halted by the bobbies, he was probably long gone. He had fired two clean shots from across that busy street, hitting Dom in the right eye and chest. The shooter had disappeared, and we were all left standing there in disbelief.

It seemed as if the entire force from Scotland Yard had shown up within the next 10 minutes. Those of us who had been close to Dom had been ushered into the security building and sat there not saying a word. We couldn't even look at each other, as if by some means, this was our fault. We should have invited his bodyguard, we shouldn't have drunk so much, we should have left earlier, we should have left later, we shouldn't have invited him at all. Then there was the guilt in wondering if we could have prevented it or seen it coming or somehow saved him. I was wondering why I hadn't chased down the killer and shot him. All of these thoughts were ludicrous, of course, but brought on by human nature.

When the door opened, we all looked up. Inspector O'Neil walked in, took a slow look around the room and his gaze landed on me. He sighed and shook his head. Everyone else turned to look at me. He methodically went around the room, asking individuals to accompany him into another room. He asked the routine questions to build a picture of what happened, taking copious notes, repeating questions occasionally from different perspectives to ensure accuracy and help jog our already fuzzy memories. No surprise, he asked me in last. As I took a seat, O'Neil said, "We need to stop meeting like this, you and I. At this point, I feel like we should be opening a bottle of bourbon to share a drink as old friends." This could have been a joke, but he was not laughing. He had another dead body on his hands, no killer, and me just happening to be around at both killings. And then there was that occurrence of the break in at my hotel room. I had managed to get myself mixed up in a situation I had no desire to be involved in.

I answered his standard questions about what I had seen and heard this evening, as had everyone else. The Inspector was very methodical in his approach to us all. After making my official state-ment, I decided it was time that I should share everything that I had seen and heard since my arrival in London with the good inspector. He was silent through my story, writing down every detail I men-tioned. He then asked what seemed like dozens of questions for more details to fill in gaps. We went through this for over an hour. There was no question his mind that the shooter was the same who had killed the henchman earlier. The signature shot to the eye could have only been accomplished by a professional sniper. And one who was very proud of his marksmanship, to boot. The henchman had to have been shot as he turned to look behind him. Not much time for a shooter to aim and shoot. Ballistics on the ammunition would confirm this theory. In both cases, the shooter made no attempt to cover his tracks and the kills were definitely not made to look like accidents, so O'Neil was pretty sure that it was not a local. This was a hired shooter who stayed off the grid when not working. Of course, none of this tied the hotel room incident into these murders, but it seemed too coincidental. Especially since I had not met either of the victims at the time. One unanswered question that was bothersome, "Had the shooter seen me look his way?" O'Neil asked me to stop by the station tomorrow and said if I remembered anything else, be sure to write it down and bring it with me.

10

$\mathcal{F}$inding the $\mathcal{K}$iller

O n the streets of London, I had personally witnessed two street killings. One on Oxford Street after I had left Burberry's, the other when our friend Dom Gloriosos was shot right outside the Wimbledon main gate.

It was a hot, hazy, drizzly morning as we all gathered around the coffin at the cemetery. Dom was a devout catholic, so we decided to absent ourselves from the long church ceremony prior to the graveside service. Frank and I attended Dom's funeral along with a great many others. Perhaps even the killer was in the crowd. There were too many people there to tell. I noticed that the Russian crime boss was among a group that seemed to be comprised of various ethnic backgrounds, probably leaders of lesser gangs and organizations, all come to pay their respects to a fallen, but well respected, rival. This seemed to irritate Inspector O'Neil, who was also present, probably hoping for one individual boss he could point his finger at. I spent my time consoling Dom's young girlfriend, who was holding up with tear filled eyes and sobs, polite half smiles to words of condolences and uncomfortable glances at the coffin in front of her. When the Priest said the words, "From dust you are and to dust you shall return," the emotions finally overcame her, and she buried her head in my shoulder as she cried uncontrollably for the remainder of the service. She managed to compose herself enough to lay a single red rose on the coffin as they prepared to lower it into the grave. I helped her to the limo, tucked her into the seat with a soft kiss on her forehead, and closed the door. I watched as the car pulled away and started down the drive. The softness of the skin I had kissed lingered on my lips. Frank appeared at my side and looked at me as if to say "What?" I just shook my head and turned to head back to his car.

On the way to the car, we intercepted Inspector O'Neil and asked if we could come and talk with him…we wanted to see how his investigation into Dom's untimely death was going. It was still early, so he suggested we stop by later that afternoon. According to O'Neill Dom had a lot of enemies and potential enemies—-the most obvious being the Russians. The police did not have much to go on and they hadn't found the man in the dark jacket who had been following me and whom I had seen fleeing the shooting scene. O'Neill did say Dom was killed with a Browning automatic, the same gun that had killed the man who ran into me in the street, and that they were looking for the gun. Not surprisingly, all of the registered owners of that type of firearm came up clean. O'Neil was certain that our killer was a hired hand brought in for a few quick jobs. He was hoping the culprit was already on his way home. He didn't need any more dead bodies.

After meeting with the inspector, Frank and I decided we would make a few enquiries ourselves. Little did we know…we would be under scrutiny from both the Russians, Dom's own henchmen and the police. We made an appointment to see Yuri with the excuse that Frank wanted to re-negotiate his shop lease. We also wanted to talk with him about our betting suggestion as a way for Frank to get out of his original lease.

I met Yuri Grosegann only once before. He would entertain Russian tennis players before Wimbledon. He appeared about sixty years old but may have been younger. He had a scar on his chin with one eye watering all the time and would rub it as he talked. He would always be accompanied by two of his henchmen. All were finely dressed, with the overbearing signature gold chains around the neck and gold and diamond rings on their massive hands.

Frank, when he started his original sports stores in London, bought the storefronts from Grosegann, with suspiciously favorable leasing terms. The one catch was that Frank had to pay a monthly protection fee, in exchange for required 'security'. As the years went by this arrangement really bothered Frank; however, as with almost all businesses in the east end, this was the accepted thing that had to be done. When Frank purchased and built-up other stores, he made sure now to do all his business in other parts of London. However, further development meant capital expenditures beyond what a single store was positioned to finance. His established relationship with the Russians made them the easiest route for financing to fill the gap. Plus, when they discovered his plans to expand, they somewhat insisted on "helping him out". Now, he wanted badly to get out from under the reach of the Russians, sooner, rather than later.

Wimbledon was the only major tennis event where local bookmakers were allowed by the government to operate. This had been policy for years. When Bobby Riggs played Wimbledon only one year, in 1939 he bet on himself to win the triple through a friend placing his bet with a local bookmaker. When he won the singles, doubles and mixed doubles he pocketed over a hundred thousand pounds. Riggs never returned to Wimbledon.

Frank Brown was one of those ambitious, honest, fun-loving workaholics. Rising from a working-class background with little formal education, he had used his personal charisma and contacts to expand his sports agent and sporting goods businesses into a prominent position in Britain. Frank enjoyed a reputation as a genuine and honest businessman. When he asked me, as his friend if I would be willing to throw my tennis match at Wimbledon for a big cash payday, I was shocked and insulted. This was not the Frank that I knew and had come to be close friends with. I stammered out a resounding "NO, don't be absurd! How could you ever believe that I would be agreeable to something like that? I can't believe you would even think up something like that!" At that point I realized that he wouldn't. "This isn't you, is it? It's coming from your debt to the Russians, isn't it?" Frank explained that if I was to do this, it would release him from his longtime commitment to the Russians. As the Russians controlled several of the prominent bookmakers, Yuri Grosegann could make this work. But there had to be another way.

Our friend Michael Stich was a surprise winner of Wimbledon the previous year. Since then, he had got married and struggled a bit with his tennis. However, he came into Wimbledon, seeded #5. Leading up to Wimbledon, I practiced with him several times. He clearly was not in the same aggressive form as last year... I was beating him in practice sets. When we finished practice the week before the draw came out Frank came by and I offhandedly said that he should put his money on whoever he plays in the first round. We checked with Uri's bookmaker and yes Michael was at 10—1 odds. When the draw came out, he was scheduled to play Yusef el Amin of Egypt, who was a late qualifier and an unknown on Tuesday on Center Court, at 80-1 odds. The previous year's champion always plays on Center Court on the first day of men's singles, the Tuesday. The ladies champion always played first on the first day of competition, the Monday. We checked around. Amin had won two grass qualifiers over the last weeks. We decided to put some cash on the Egyptian... I suggested Frank do Yuri a favor and tell him to back Amin.

The misty drizzle continued into the afternoon as we went up the steps. We entered Yuri's front office to be greeted by his secretary, a dark Jamaican beauty with very ample breasts and long dark legs. She wore a yellow short sleeved blouse, unbuttoned just enough. Her black skirt fell midway across her thighs. She opened the doors to Uri's office to announce our arrival.

He went to the window, lit a cigarette, and took a sip of his hot black tea. London rain drizzled through the early fog outside. He gazed down at the park outside. Yuri Grosegann crushed out his cigarette and finished his tea, as we stood just outside his office. He was a large well-muscled, stocky man of about fifty, dyed hair to cover the grey, with a neatly trimmed moustache. He wore nothing but the best suits, had impeccable, manicured, very clean white hands. His parents had come to Britain with nothing. He had inherited the east London connection from his deceased father. He and his younger accountant brother together ran the Russian connection. Both had become very wealthy over the past ten years.

Grosegann switched on the TV in his large office as he motioned us to come in. Details of Dom's funeral were front and center. Everyone knew that Dom was the longtime crime boss of the east end. He was, as it turns out, a very generous man to his church, his friends, and as we knew, a congenial host at his house and on his yacht. He was very popular despite his ruthless shortcomings. The police really did not relish trying to solve this murder.

We entered his office. As we sat down, he poured himself a generous tumbler of twenty-year-old Appleton Jamaican dark rum. His first comment was, "A crime that you can't even enjoy a simple evening at a sports event without getting shot!! What is the world coming to?" Yuri had been a good-looking young man, it appeared, but he had gone soft and fleshy with too much alcohol and rich food. He wore a smart Saville Row striped dark blue suit, with a light blue silk tie and white shirt. His eyes were bloodshot and puffy. His posture was erect with a commanding stance. He looked very sure of himself. We refrained from responding to his comment.

Business appeared very good for Yuri and his organization. He sat behind a large mahogany desk with some fine artworks on the wall. He pointed us to a large watercolor of his Jamaican plantation house. He drove a large black Rolls Royce with one of his 'boys' as chauffeur. He always sat in the back seat with his main bodyguard.

Frank started right into his problem about the debt on his property. He had brought me along to vouch for the fact that Michael Stich, the previous year's champion could lose in the first round. I said my piece about his opponent, the Egyptian and that I had already bet on him to win. Yuri seemed encouraged by what I had to say, "You practiced with Stich?" and I said he was beatable in his first match when the grass was very green, slick and slippery. The weather promised to be cold and dreary which gave our proposition more credence. He said he would check around through his sources and get back to us. As we were leaving, we observed Uri's highly polished black Rolls parked outside, an eerie reminder of the opulence of the top dons of London's underworld. A burly black chauffeur sat in the driver's seat. Pretty soon Uri's gorgeous black Jamaican secretary emerged, got in the back seat, her black silky skirt rising above her knees as she got in. She opened her black Gucci handbag, lit up a Benson and Hedges and was quickly whisked away.

We left, thinking that was it. Back at Frank's place we were showering and having a cold Carlsberg before dinner when Yuri called. He said his bookmaker would take a large bet for him, probably intimidated by the ruthless Russian. Frank was pleased that Yuri put a bundle on our pick, then after he stalled for a minute, he said "let's hope we are right on this". We decided to put together what we had on the bet with Yuri's bookmaker the next day. I called Mirium that night, and she wanted in too. She said she would cash in some of her South African diamonds tomorrow—" and let's have a bit of fun with this". I also called my mate and doubles partner Aaron Wasson and clued him in on the deal—he always had some ready cash stashed away available for a good opportunity. Frank and I would follow that first match with special interest.

That evening Frank took me to his favorite Indian place for dinner. We drank Stag Indian larger from those huge bottles, then went over to Dom's club in Knightsbridge for a bit of fun. Dom's girl was there, and she latched onto my arm as soon as we arrived. We took one of Dom's best tables, she sat right up close to me rubbing my thigh. The club was dark and smoky with the only light from sconces on the walls and fake candlelight on the tables.

Frank had given a very short, elegant speech at graveside. He had quoted the Roman General and poet Catullus "So forever, brother, hail and farewell". Dom's girl teared up and said how much she appreciated the fact that we chose to be there. She was young and appeared very athletic, with fluid moves on the dance floor. Frank described her as a "young deer let run free", a bit young for me, but seriously gorgeous. She was sending very discreet, but clear, signals that she was looking for male companionship and was hoping I would oblige. When she looked my way, her incredible, large brown eyes seemed to light up. She had a perfectly formed body, small, upturned breasts, small, graceful wrists and strong, slender arms and legs. She smelled of vanilla and blossoms from some kind of flower. I was smitten already.

Her name was Susan. We had a drink at our table and as we were leaving, she leaned over and put a key and a note in my hand. "Go there, I will be home shortly after midnight." I didn't feel the need to mention this to Frank. We decided we were feeling like being somewhere a bit more low-keyed after the funeral of a friend and went to a local pub, with a fine selection of ales, where we could either talk or not. Around 11pm I excused myself, saying I was going to visit a friend. Frank knew better than to pry and left it with "I'll see you tomorrow."

Her modest, but well appointed, second floor flat was on the other side of the Thames off a small, enclosed courtyard. I turned the key and went in. The door opened into a living and dining area, with a comfortable looking dark grey sofa, and matching chair with an ottoman. The table in front of the sofa had a single orchid plant which was blooming in shades of purple. A small table between the chair and sofa had a modern style lamp, several travel magazines and a music box, the rug was a pale combination of blues and greens. There was a modern, glass top dining table with blonde wood legs behind the sofa, with cushioned seating for six, with a faux flower arrangement as decoration. A hutch in matching wood, with displayed dishes and glassware was along the side wall of the apartment. The remainder of the wall was taken up by an opening leading, I assumed to the bedroom and bath, and a long, ebony colored buffet/bar, well supplied with some top shelf liquors and a full wine cooler. The scene looked as if everything was purchased out of a furniture showroom display. The kitchen was off to the left, separated from the living space by a high counter. After rummaging through the fridge, I fixed myself some eggs and toast and helped myself to a port from the bar. I went to the window at the end of the room and looked out. The murky brown waters of the river flowed sluggishly by. The apartment had that sweet vanilla fragrance she wore.

She arrived shortly after midnight and was obviously glad to see me. It has been said that grief can be a powerful aphrodisiac. I was inclined to believe that at this moment. She quickly came into my arms and initiated a long and passionate kiss. She took my hand and led me straight into her bedroom hastily pulling my clothes off as we circled the bed. This was too good to be true; just what I needed and apparently her, too. Her hair was like silk on my body as she roughly pushed me down onto the bed and made her way on top of me, covering me with warm, moist kisses from her soft, full lips, like flicks from a flame that couldn't be quenched, setting my body on fire. It was a night of utter abandonment and passion, fueled by the intense emotions pent up from the occurrences of the last few weeks. I had planned on this being nothing more than a distraction, but there was something about her, a vulnerability that came through in the little conversation we had, that drew me in, and I was beginning to think it might be more.

I met Frank the next morning, and we headed out looking for answers to Dom's death. London traffic was like being in a plastic bag that became tighter the more you struggled. I was hot, with no air conditioning. Frank and I started to think about possible suspects. The actual shooter, as O'Neil had pointed out, was probably an expatriate, and we would never see him again. The real question was, who hired him and why? What does Dom's bodyguard think? What does Dom's girlfriend think? It seemed like everyone in London had theories, fueled by an active press. We decided to interview Dom's old bodyguard to see if Dom had confided in him or if he had seen or heard anything that might give a clue. Even if justice couldn't be served since nothing would tie the murder back to the source, Frank and I needed closure on the death of a friend.

From Knightsbridge, Frank and I ventured down the narrow back lanes. They were dirty with open drains and the stink of urine. The streetwalkers were out in their gaudy outfits. We ventured into a pub that looked like it had not been cleaned for years. It had the smell of old wood, aged leather, stale cigars and stale booze. It had definitely seen better days, like an old worn suit with holes in it. This is where Frank had arranged to meet Dom's old bodyguard. Scanning the dark room, it took a bit for our eyes to adjust, and even then, we could barely make out Mario. He sat off to one side in a dark corner table. We were hopeful Dom's long-term bodyguard would be able to point to who would have wanted Dom out of the way, enough to arrange his murder.

A scruffy waiter who looked like he might have emerged from the very woodwork, he blended in so well with the character of the establishment, brought us Russian style black tea in old, dirty looking glasses with ornate metal holders. Mario said it was clear that both street murders were connected and word on the street was there was a foreign shooter in town. The only reason for someone to hire out these kills was to make absolutely certain there was no connection back to them and that there were no slip-ups. His money was on the Russians. and said he was investigating through his underground connections. He took Frank's phone number and said he would call him when he learns something. We left having gained very little.

The next morning, it was drizzling and foggy again. I sat down with coffee and started to read the papers. "Did you read this" I asked. The Times had an expose' on the two murders. The author of the article, James Madigan was a notable Wimbledon journalist. As his focus this week was on The Championships, it was not surprising that he attributed the murders to some wagers that were to be made on Wimbledon matches. "This is a completely new angle—we need to talk to him". Later that morning, Frank and I found Madigan at a small coffee shop in Wimbledon Village on Church Road. We indicated that as Dom was a friend, and the fact that I had been witness to the first killing, plus we were both involved in Wimbledon, we were very curious as to why he thought the killings were related to Wimbledon wagers. This was the morning of the Michael Stich match that we had bet a bundle on along with the Russians. We were actually concerned that we had put our friend Michael in danger by our conversation with Yuri. We were basing our confidence on knowledge of the game, and it hadn't occurred to us that Yuri might not feel that that was enough insurance—had the Russians pressured Stich into losing today? Had they threatened his girlfriend?

I had to put all of this aside. I needed to prepare myself for my first match at Wimbledon. My doubles partner Aaron Wasson and I had made the draw and had less than two days to prepare before our first match.

11

The Money Match

The cool breeze picked up as we took our seats in the player's box in the grandstand on Center Court. A few pigeons circled around to the back of the stand, almost as though they were waiting for the first match to start. I could tell Frank was nervous. This was the traditional day and time when last year's Gentleman's Champion would play his first match. Frank fidgeted in his seat with white knuckles on his knees. The linesmen and umpire emerged from the darkness of the tunnel into a gloomy dry but grey day and took their places. Next, at precisely 2.05pm the players appeared. The Egyptian, Ismail El Sharif emerged first to a smattering of polite applause. As our friend and defending champion, Michael Stich emerged into the daylight…the crowd erupted. Center Court was only about half full at this time. It was a bit early yet for a full crowd, but the noise was loud. Most of the upper crust Royal Box holders in their suits and ties and expensive summer dresses were not in their seats yet, having the last of their strawberries and cream in the member's preferred enclosure.

Ismail el Sharif was a tall, lanky dark Arab who had some serious weapons. If he was having a good day, he could beat almost anyone with his spin serve and great probing forehand. He came to the net with confidence and could play explosive tennis if he wanted to. He was a world class squash player and consequently was 'fit as a fiddle' as the pom's say. I played him at squash last year in Australia and he 'cleaned my clock'. He had won two qualifying matches already so was used to the slick grass.

Michael Stich, the defending champion had played his best tennis ever last year to beat some of the top players, including fellow German Boris Becker in the final. Never before had there been an all-German final at Wimbledon, and never before had Michael Stich produced a performance like the one he fashioned that day. Michael's second serve returns, his consistent serving games, and the penetration of his backhand and passes to beat his countryman and three-time former champion, in an absorbing battle of wills. Although the handsome six-footer had had a somewhat mediocre year, and had got married, he had high hopes to repeat on his favorite surface.

Stich started off slowly, slipping badly on the slick grass in the first game, losing his serve. El Sharif ran out the set holding serve fairly easily. In the second set, Stich appeared to recover some, breaking the Egyptian in his first service game.

A breeze picked up against Stich's serve—he lost that game and pretty soon it was 5-4 in the second set with the Egyptian serving. El Sharif had a long wobbly serving game but put his nervousness aside enough to close out the second set with a flashy ace. Two sets to zero Egypt! We were looking good. It looked like a big payday may be due. We were now on the edge of our seats. The third set was a close tussle with Sharif getting nervous. At 3-3 in the third he choked an easy volley into the net to go down game point. However, Stich slipped badly again and had to take a time out. He appeared badly shaken. The trainer came on court and taped up his upper thigh.

For the rest of the set Michael walked and ran with a slight limp. It looked like a hamstring pull to us. The Egyptian now gained confidence with every point, probing his heavy shots wide and out of Michael's reach. The crowd stirred, sensing a big upset. Michael Stich, the defending champion was in trouble, and in danger of losing in the first round.

Brenda appeared very fidgety, almost crying, crossing her legs often. When Michael slipped again, she resigned herself to the loss. El Sharif, drawing on his squash winning ways, served out the third set for one of the biggest upsets in Wimbledon history. Frank and I were of course ecstatic, reserving our celebration for when we got home. We had quite a payday and so did the Russian. A couple of days later, the Russian boss showed his class by returning the deed on Frank's store, much to Frank's great relief. We vowed to keep it quiet about the bet and our great success—after all Michael was our friend. However, I sensed his decline, never again rising to that same level of success. That was my last wager on a tennis match.

12

The Killer Caught

My first-round match was against Roger Randall. Randall was ranked 15th in the world and seeded 12th at Wimbledon. He was a 6'4" flashy and handsome Englishman with a huge serve and big forehand. He was the big hope of the Brits for Wimbledon. They had not had a Wimbledon Men's singles champion since Fred Perry won three times in the 30's; they were eager for success and had recently embarked on an ambitious junior development program. Randall's father was in the House of Lords so the press treated him with kid gloves. He was especially well liked by women, young and old.

We were scheduled to play on Court 16, not one of the main show courts, which was good as this would limit his very supportive crowd. He would come out on court, from the shade of the stands to the bright noon sunshine, his long oiled black hair, slicked down tightly. Earlier I had looked at my reflection in the glass of the locker room door. I had on my 'all white' Fred Perry warmup with my new wool cricket sweater around my shoulders. I felt pretty good that day as I was to meet Mirium again before the match. Wimbledon had an 'all white' clothing rule, so all competitors were required to wear white—no exemptions. Frank had arranged for me to receive a large allocation of whites prior to Wimbledon week.

Mirium met me outside the locker room. We were to have an early lunch on the Wimbledon member's veranda courtesy of Roger Ambrose, the Secretary of the All England Club and were to meet with the Australian Ambassador to London and the Chancellor of the University of London. Mirium wore a pale bone colored pantsuit with her diamonds and a very subdued string of Mikimoto pearls around her neck. She looked very classy and at home. I was glad she was with me. The ambassador was newly appointed to London and expressed the wishes of all Australians for my participation and success. The Chancellor was there to express the support of my follow students and my professors—Talk about pressure!

The pigeons were there waiting for us. It was a gloomy afternoon as we made our way through the crowd to court 16. There was a large crowd waiting for us as Andre Agassi had played there right before us-the crowd was overflowing. This was Agassi's first and only match on grass for several years... He had chosen to skip Wimbledon. He didn't like grass. He said, "grass is for cows" and the press took him literally. The remaining crowd was mostly comprised of young women, when they saw it was to be the dashing dark Englishman Randall on court next.

Mirium came with me, looking as regal and relaxed as ever, took her seat in the player's box with Frank. The remainder of the seats around court 16 were taken up by women, young, old and in between. The handsome Roger Randall was about to put on a show for them. The stands, built to accommodate 1,500 spectators had about 2,000 screaming women, hanging or standing at every possible vantage point. We had a full team of ball boys, who were very eager, having been training for weeks for this occasion. After the on-court warmup, the umpire said "ready, play". Randall won the first point amid ravenous screams...this was going to be a circus! My concentration was completely shot. I really only had two spectators, Mirium and Frank. I said to Frank at the change of ends. "blimey mate, this is a zoo!"

However, I was ready to make a match of it, even if outnumbered and outranked. My doubles partner Aaron Wasson, showed up after the first set, making it three for me versus the crowd. British television stations were featuring the match as Randall was Britain's main hope for the title. As we got to 5-5 in the second set, and I was walking back to the serve position, I glanced at the stands and I couldn't believe my eyes! There in the stands, just three rows in at an aisle seat, was the same dark man whom I had seen following me several times before Dom's murder, and whom I saw rushing from the shooters position immediately following the shot that killed Dom. He was without the leather hoodie in this heat, but I would never forget that profile and posture. I called for play to stop and walked over to Frank, who was looking very confused. I told him I was worried, why, and to get O'Neill here, now! No surprise, I lost the second set 7-5...the crowd went wild. I was too distracted, keeping my eye on the man who was likely not just the killer, but may be targeting me, sitting right there in front of me, cool as a cucumber. I knew O'Neil would be on the grounds, and I knew he would show up within moments with security police. At that point I had nothing to lose, after all this man might be there to kill me. I stopped play for a second time and ran right up into the stands. Frank saw me make my move and ran to block the aisle so the man wouldn't be able run in the other direction. The killer saw me approaching and stood to leave, but Frank was approaching from the other direction by then. The sight of Frank was enough to make him hesitate just a moment. Enough time for me to reach him. I was in front of him, eyeball to eyeball as he turned back towards me. It was then or never. I couldn't give him a chance to get away before O'Neil got there. I punched him right square in the mouth, knocking him down into the seats, before he had a chance to react. Let me tell you that was a good punch, seen around the world in all the newspapers and on every television screen that night. O'Neill came rushing through the crowd, subdued him and hauled him away in handcuffs.

When I went to pick up my racket to resume play, I realized my right wrist hurt like hell. Before resuming, I got it taped and then continued the match as best I could... One thing for sure, the crowd were now very much for me. I made a good show of it but lost in four sets. In my mind, I didn't lose at all. I walked out of there, alive, and knew that Dom's killer had been brought in.

Later we all met with O'Neill. He said he had searched this man's car and apartment. The apartment was furnished and had a short-term lease under the name Don Johnson. Obviously an alias. There were no documents identifying the man for who he really was, or where he was from. He said there was a slip of paper with the name and address of the first victim as well as several pages on Dom. Possibly the papers we thought might have been retrieved from my hotel room my first night there. They also found photos with all of us who had been around Dom the week before his death. Forensics were checking the place for anything that would tie the killer to whoever hired him, but first appearances told O'Neill they wouldn't find anything. Scotland Yard matched the Baretta found hidden in his apartment with the bullet that killed the first victim and Dom. O'Neill noted how foolish and dangerous my move at the tennis match was, but still thanked me for trapping the killer.

The next morning papers were very explicit. 'Aussie captures Killer at Wimbledon—Game, Set and Match'. The papers included an interview and explanation with O'Neill and a headline of 'Hardigan wins over crowd by punching killer'. I was a big hero!

After all that excitement and the interviews in the press room after, I was exhausted. I had a doubles match in two days and opted at Mirium's suggestion for a quiet night with room service and her there to console me.

13

Kidnapped

The next morning after my highly unconventional singles match, I arose early and as I rolled over in bed with my wonderful Mirium next to me, a pleasant sigh softly escaped her lips. "Yesterday was quite a day" she said in that sleepy kind of voice that lies somewhere in the realm of not awake, but not quite asleep either. I softly kissed her shoulder and quietly got out of bed, so as not to bring her fully awake. After taking a shower and dressing, I ventured out into the cold, coppery light of morning. Mirium had awakened enough to say goodbye and confirm what I had already guessed. She had elected to stay in bed and said she would meet me at the Queen's Club after the practice I had scheduled with Frank and Aaron late morning. We needed to prepare for the doubles match. Susan had called and left a message for me to come by her flat when I could. I still had her key.

I opted for the 20-minute walk to find some coffee and a light breakfast over on Oxford St. The streets were beginning to become congested with everyone heading off to their daily grind. Even at this early hour, a steady stream of commuters could be seen heading down to the underground, otherwise referred to as "the tube", at each station entrance I passed. I just couldn't get myself to refer to it as the tube. That name just conjures up visions of gerbils in a never-ending maze. I found a small café with an empty table near the window and picked up a paper on my way in. I got in line to order my coffee and couldn't resist the fresh baked scones with Devonshire cream and strawberry jam. The aroma of the fresh ground coffee was heavy in the air I took a deep breath in to thoroughly enjoy it. Since most of the patrons were just grabbing coffees to go on their way to work, the table that beckoned me in was still available when I picked up my order. I sat down to relish a sense of normalcy, peace and quiet with my paper and coffee. The sun was peeking through between two buildings and briefly bathed me in it's warm light. This was a good morning!

I decided to head over to the Queen's club early, so I took the underground rather than a cab. It was not as comfortable a ride as a cab, but in daytime traffic, much quicker. I picked up the train from the Bond Street Station heading to Green Park, changed trains to take the Piccadilly Line over to Baron's Court. From there it was a short walk to the Training center at the Queen's club. After all of the media coverage of my involvement in the capture of Dom's killer, we chose to practice here to avoid the press and well-wishers likely to be on the lookout for me at Wimbledon. At least for the moment, I was a bit of a celebrity, and a Wimbledon competitor to boot. It was hard to keep a low profile, but arriving at our practice early avoided some of the unwanted attention. Other players at the club were congratulatory and full of questions, which I managed to dodge by insisting that I had to tend to my wrist before practice. That was a matter that they understood. Being there early allowed me time to have an ultrasound treatment for my still sore wrist and have it carefully taped to avoid any further injury. It was feeling pretty good by the time Frank and Aaron arrived. Frank, being Frank, had all the gear and clothes I needed for practice. We headed out to the courts and the instant our feet left the hard surface of the sidewalk, our focus was on tennis and tennis only—the feel of the grass, the rackets in our hands, the net, and of course—the ball.

It felt good to get back on court with my good mates and to sweat out the tension and excitement of yesterday. Running on the grass was essential therapy—something I realized I would truly miss when I had to go back to school in September. It was highly unlikely, though, that I could convince the school board to put in a grass court, but it was a nice thought.

By the time we finished, Mirium was sitting in the stands waiting for me. I quickly showered and excused myself from Frank and Aaron's company, scoffing at the good-natured ribbing about my relationship with "an older woman" and how "my life is no longer my own". They did have to admit that they, too, would choose Mirium's company over their own.

I climbed the stairs to the seat next to Mirium. She looked a bit distressed. She started the conversation with "I'm so sorry". I felt my stomach clench, as I couldn't imagine what was coming next. She went on to explain that she had gotten a call from a friend in Northampton whose husband had suffered a massive heart attack. She had asked if Mirium could come spend a couple of days with her. She was one of those women who totally relied on her husband for everything and really didn't know how to cope with everything the medical people were throwing her way. She desperately needed the strength that she had always found when Mirium was there to lean on. My stomach relaxed and I let out a sign of relief. I took her hand and let her know I understood. Australians know the importance of 'mates' and the meaning of friendship. I absolutely insisted that she go to be with her friend. She said she would like to make the 3:15 train out of Euston Station so she would miss the commuter crowds and get to Northampton with less stops. Frank and Aaron had already left, so we walked back up to Baron's Court and caught a taxi back to the hotel.

We had a somewhat long lunch in the hotel bar, as she talked a bit about her past antics, when she and her friend were younger, growing up together. We made tentative plans for her return. She was confident that we would be in the finals for the doubles match. She would likely be returning to Winston Gardens before getting back in time for our final match. We went up to the room to get her luggage, called for a taxi to Euston Station and sat in the lobby for our ride to arrive. Traffic was pleasantly light, so we arrived at the station early. We sat and had coffee and some delightful chocolates at a café on the balcony overlooking the main concourse. When it came time for her to go to her train, she promised to call the next evening to see how our matches went. She also hoped to have firmed up her plans for returning to London. We embraced and took our time on a goodbye kiss in the crowded main concourse. She headed to her train and I exited the main entrance. I paused just outside, thinking about what I would do with the rest of my evening. Susan's invitation was still open, but she wouldn't be off work until midnight.

The heat of the afternoon was oppressive after being in the air-conditioned building, and I thought of heading up to Hampstead Heath's Men's Bathing Pond. I wouldn't need a suit as long as I stayed on the nude bathing side. Very different culture than in America, where you needed to hide off in some remote mountain stream or quarry if you wanted to take a dip in the buff. Here you could feel totally comfortable in the midst of the city. The Women's pond, on the other hand, did not allow nude bathing, much to the disappointment of the men of London. The water in the pond is very cold, even this time of year. In spring, swimmers find the need to 'habituate' themselves to the water, spending gradually more time in it at each visit. I decided to go for a quick dip. It was too hot and humid to walk the few miles, so I headed over to the taxi stand. Ten minutes later I was walking along the wooded path to the bath house and was momentarily reminded of walking in the outback with my Dad, as a kid. The memory was snatched from me by the sound of someone or something crashing through the brush towards me. I froze in my tracks wondering if I should flee, just as a dog came bounding through the woods, followed by his owner desperately trying to retrieve the pup who had gotten free from his leash. I let out the breath I was holding, tried to calm my racing heartbeat and laughed at my overactive imagination. I got to the pond and slowly eased into the seemingly frigid water. Despite the heat, there were very few bathers. One advantage of being able to visit when others were at work. I kept my right arm submerged to allow the cold to penetrate the slight swelling that was still prevailing in my wrist. As I got acclimated to the water, my whole body was responding to the therapeutic cold. When I was sufficiently numb, I laid out on the grass to dry off. The heat, at least for a few moments felt wonderful on my skin.

I moved to a shaded spot to prevent a bad sunburn and must have dozed off. When I opened my eyes, the shadows were much longer as the sun was much lower in the sky. This was not somewhere I wanted to be as it got dark.

I walked back in the direction of the Parliament Hill tennis courts and cut over to the bus stop on Highgate Rd. I didn't have to wait for the bus, as a taxi was just cruising by and with a sharp whistle, I was able to hail it down. I was amazed at my good luck. Seemed too good to be true, actually. The driver was an Irishman this time. Not what one would expect in London at this time of unrest. He also looked a bit more rugged than your normal driver. I dismissed it as I remembered my imagination run amuck with my encounter with the dog. Plus, not all Irishman were in agreement with the terrorist tactics. He glanced at me in the rearview a few times, before asking if I was "that famous tennis player who nailed that gangster's killer?" He had seen my picture on the news. "Nice pluck!" which I took to be a compliment on my punch. We continued with the usual conversation. He asked where I had planned to have dinner. I told him I wasn't sure yet, but somewhere in the vicinity of Oxford St. I had him drop me off at my hotel for a shower and change of clothes. This heat makes this routine before dinner an absolute necessity. The driver already had his radio in hand, I presume to call for his next ride, as I paid the fare. He offered to return to pick me up for dinner, which I thought very considerate of him, but turned down the offer since I knew if he had picked up a big fare between now and when I was ready, I could end up waiting a long time for him to show.

It was still early enough for a walk through Hyde Park before going for dinner. I cut across through Kensington Gardens, then followed along the Serpentine before heading towards the Marble Arch and Oxford St. The temperatures even at twilight were still around 90 degrees Fahrenheit. People gathered in the park, all shapes, sizes and backgrounds. Many were lounged on the chaise lounges along the serpentine, trying to catch a cool breeze. Many were well heeled shoppers taking a break from the upscale stores along Oxford Street. The previous driver had recommended a new Indian Restaurant on Portman Mews S and I thought I'd give it a try. I thought it would be an easy walk until I got one block in on Oxford and found myself shoulder to shoulder with hundreds of others in the crowded street. As I waded through the crowd, I thought I recognized the Irish brogue of my driver that afternoon close behind me. Once again, my imagination was getting in the way of reason. I turned onto Portman St. and left most of the crowd behind. A good and a bad thing. While there were less people, those that were along the road were not 'my type'. I was approaching an intersection with Granville Pl. where there were several commercial vans parked along the street. I lowered my gaze to the path to be as inconspicuous as possible but as I was passing the corner, I couldn't help but notice a sight that was offensive to my sensibilities. It was a sight seen in that part of London at that time, all too often. I was so uncomfortable by the sight, that I stopped suddenly, thinking maybe I should return to the obscurity of the crowds on Oxford St. There were, in plain sight, two men in leather jackets groping each other in the semi darkness against the side of a dark green delivery van. In the split second that I had stopped, I was attacked from behind. One hand covered my mouth while the other held a knife at my throat. A clear deep Irish voice ordered me not to try and fight, just cooperate and I wouldn't be hurt. Another man joined the first, this voice I recognized. It was the driver I had earlier and thought I was imagining things when I heard him behind me on Oxford St. The two men dragged me into the back of the van, being careful not to let me see their faces. Tape was stuck over my mouth and a hood was dropped over my head. My hands and ankles were quickly bound. I was left lying on a blanket on the hard floor of the van as it sped off. My mind was reeling. It all happened so quickly. I had no idea who these men were, or what they wanted from me. The road noise prevented me from clearly hearing what little conversation the two men had. The van I was in smelled of grease and oil, like an automotive shop. It was a very bumpy, harrowing ride through the London streets. Lying on the floor, hooded, I could only use my hearing and smell to try to guess where I was going. At first, I could tell by the turns that we headed south along Hyde Park, then went past Buckingham Palace towards Westminster Bridge. I was able to hear the quarter bells of Big Ben when we were stopped for a traffic light and I could feel the expansion joints as we went over the bridge. We then went over some train tracks, which I assume were at Waterloo station. After that we were in an area that I was totally unfamiliar with. We made numerous turns, went over more tracks, then went through what sounded like a rather long tunnel, so I assumed that we crossed the Thames at least once more. When we exited the tunnel, it seemed like we were going in a large loop back around on ourselves. For what seemed like forever, it felt like we were on what the Brits call a motorway—highway driving with no traffic lights. When we finally exited off that road, we made a few turns on some rough roads in what I imagined to be an industrial area. When the van finally stopped the two men got out and called out to someone. I heard a door open and slam closed as a third man responded, "Leg it! Me mot is up to high doh!" The van door opened. the air was heavy with the smell of oil and polluted water, as if we were at a refinery or tanker loading dock. This time of night it was quiet, but I could see a lot of artificial light through my hood.

They dragged me to the van door and cut the tape on my ankles so I could walk. I vaguely heard "Don't do anything daft" as I flexed my legs and feet to get the blood flowing again. I heard an overhead door opening and I was led into a building that smelled of damp paper and concrete dust, with what felt like sand grit on the floor. It had the open space, echoing sound of a warehouse. They led me to the left, one on each side, gripping my arms with hands that had a strength that told me fleeing would be futile. The floor changed to metal and the third man closed the doors to the freight elevator we had just entered. The lift rose one floor and we exited into what I I'm guessing was more warehouse that must have had some office spaces. We moved into what seemed to be a dimly lit hallway, as the three of us couldn't stay abreast of each other. We passed through a doorway on the right and I could see light that must have been coming through a window from the outdoor lighting I had sensed when the van door opened. They switched on an overhead light and I heard a chair being dragged toward me. I was pushed down into the seat and my ankles were once again bound and taped to the chair. The tape on my wrists was removed and my wrists were taped to the arms of the chair. There was no air conditioning and the men around me reeked of old sweat. The man who had been waiting for us added the aroma of old whisky. It was difficult not to gag as they hovered over me taping me to the chair back. With my back to the door, they pulled off the hood before they left the room, at least making it easier to breathe. I could hear the lock turn. I was still gagged with tape. I was helpless. Mirium would try calling and assume that I was out having dinner or drinks with my friends. My only hope was that Frank, who was coming by the hotel in the morning to pick me up, might suspect foul play, but he would probably just assume that I had spent the night elsewhere and forgot that he was to meet me. The room they put me in must have been directly above the overhead door we entered, as I could hear large trucks coming and going downstairs as well as a few muffled Irish accents. I was pretty certain these were not standard deliveries or shipments at this time of night. I had lost a sense of time, but it must have been past midnight when the activities below me ceased. I felt as if I was smothering in the fumes from the truck exhausts but could do nothing to alleviate the situation.

Sitting there in that dark room above the garage, alone and immobilized, gave me time to think. I thought about how lucky I was to have had the opportunities I had, opportunities that I had created by hard work, persistence, and self-discipline. While in captivity sleep was hard to come by and even harder to hold on to. When I did finally doze off, I dreamed about my friends back in Sydney, and my weekends at Ocean Beach. When I awoke at one point, I thought of the quote attributed to Martha Washington, 'The greater part of our happiness or misery depends on our disposition and not on our circumstances'. A bit of a hard pill to swallow, given my current circumstances. I thought about my friends, new and old that I had spent my time in London with, about Mirium, Aaron, Joanne, our cricket team, Frank and of course Susan. I felt so flattered that such a beautiful young woman like Susan could be in love with me. I vowed right there in that cold, dark, smelly place to be a better friend. I vowed that I would complete my studies and use my talents to help others succeed. In the quiet, the adrenaline rush I had been feeding off the whole evening abruptly ended, and I succumbed to the utter exhaustion that it left behind.

In the early morning, I'm guessing just before dawn, I was jolted out of my sleep by a loud commotion below, with doors being crashed open and two shots fired. Not knowing who was involved in the confrontation, and still not knowing what my purpose here was, I became fearful that it was a rival faction and that my life may be of little value to them. As my head cleared enough to gather some semblance of awareness, I noticed the red flashing lights shining in the window. I realized that the police had arrived, and a raid was in progress below me. I used every ounce of my strength I managed to bang the chair I was in on the floor, trying to make my presence known. A few minutes later several police came crashing through the door behind me. They ran around in front of me with gun drawn. One of them turned on the lights and I blinked at the sudden brightness trying to focus. Another recognized me and blurted out, "That's Jack Hardigan, the tennis pro. He's the one who ID'd Gloriosos' killer." The officer in front of me yanked the tape covering off of my mouth, apologizing for the pain. I really didn't mind. It was just so good to be able to open my mouth. The other two cut the tape holding my chest, arms and legs. They helped me to my feet and steadied me as I got my body working again, then they helped me down the stairs to the scene below. There were about 10 police vehicles in the area in front of the building and ambulances were just arriving. Dozens of officers were gathering the apprehended criminals, two of whom had been wounded by the shots I had heard. I saw the taxi driver in one corner and identified him as one of my captors. Back from the door were the cases that had come in during the night. One of them had been opened and I could see the weapons packaged within it. It turns out that the police had placed a tracking device on one of the trucks I had heard, suspecting it of being involved in arms smuggling.

There was one prisoner being kept separate from the others. They had hit the jackpot on this raid! The leader of the activities here turned out to be Sean McNeece, a notorious Irish rebel, already a prime suspect in two recent bombings in London. Sean McNeece was a small, thin unassuming figure. Despite his unthreatening appearance in dirty grey overalls, he appeared a born leader, who was committed to his cause and a ruthless killer. I was introduced to the inspector in charge. His theory was that my involvement included them keeping me hostage in exchange for sensational publicity for their cause. Apparently, I was enough of a celebrity after the newspaper and media coverage of my encounter with Dom's killer during my first match to have caught the eye of McNeece. With the evidence they procured here and my kidnapping, McNeece and his followers would be put away for a long time. I had requested, that if it was at all possible, in this time of out of control media coverage, that the details of the kidnapping not be divulged until after the matches today. All of London would be glad to learn of McNeece's capture. The kidnapping was a small blip on the radar of that story. The murky sewers of the underworld had swallowed me up again.

I emerged pretty much unscathed, but dirty and hungry and my wrist was still sore but flexible. The EMT's did a cursory checkup on me to be sure there were no loose ends in their report. One of the officers who had freed me had made a call to notify Frank of what happened. He got there as quickly as he could. I had actually been taken to a warehouse in Dagenham, over an hour from where Frank lived. He arrived about the time that the police were securing the area and the government agents were showing up to seize the contraband. Once again, he knew not to ask questions until I was ready to talk, just expressing his disbelief and relief that I was OK. He took me back to my hotel as I filled him in on all the details on the ride back. I would have loved to get some sleep after that ordeal, but there was a doubles match that I had to be in that afternoon. I was not going to drop out after going through all of these ordeals to get here. I also wanted to get to the training room early enough for more therapy on my wrist and a proper taping.

As Frank and I drove back to my hotel, I opened the car window to take in the mid-summer humidity and let the silky softness of the air brush my skin. It was good to breathe in the warm air of the streets of London as we drove. I was glad to see Frank again after my ordeal and desperately just wanted to put this all behind me and get back to a normal routine.

Aaron showed up just as I was finishing my shower. Frank had called him and asked if he could pick up some breakfast for me and bring it with him. Said he would explain why when he got here. We filled Aaron in on the previous night's occurrence as I ate. It's amazing how good food tastes when you are legitimately hungry.

14

Doubles

Frank called for our courtesy vehicle from Queen's. It arrived promptly to take us to our doubles at Wimbledon. We stepped into a large Bentley Continental with plenty of room for all. As we drove off, the driver said, "nice press coverage" and "are you going to punch someone out today Jack? ". We all laughed, and I said, "I just hope I can get through this match with this sprained wrist." We all laughed again.

As we entered Court 4 for the doubles, my new spectators and the press were there, ready for some excitement, as well as half of Spain! We were to play the Spanish Davis Cup pair of Roig and Orantes who were great on red clay but had trouble on the slick Wimbledon grass. Also, they played 'Spanish Doubles' where they played most points from the baseline, even when serving, preferring to rely on their spinning clay court groundstrokes.

Aaron and I had an advantage here as we played 'serve and volley' tennis and we had excellent volleys and drop shots. We forced them to move up into the court where they were vulnerable. We played our best tennis in the first two sets, just like we did in the qualifier at Frinton. Aaron's sliding, lefty serve had them struggling. We were able to break them one time in each of the first two sets. At this time at Wimbledon the men's doubles was best of five sets; we were now getting tired and my wrist was killing me.

We said to each other, "we need to finish this off in three sets. We got more tired and a little anxious. However, we pulled each other along hitting good serves and volleys to finish them off in three sets. Aaron hit a deft spinning, backhand drop shot on match point, which died on the grass like a 'fried egg on a hot pan'.

Our next match was to be against the Knight brothers, Billy and John, who I knew well and had practiced with often. They were Britain's best so we figured we would be playing on one of the show courts, maybe Center Court.

The Knight brothers were sons of a member of the House of Lords and had been sent to all the right schools for gentlemen. John, the younger of the two, had boyish good looks and spoke with a typical upper-class Cambridge accent. Billy was older and much rougher looking than his brother and was clearly the leader of the team with the more powerful forehand and serve. This British team was a throwback to past eras when only gentlemen played on the hallowed grounds of Wimbledon. There were some players during the early years who challenged these class distinctions. One of the first to do this was Anthony Wilding, son of a New Zealand sheep farmer, attended Cambridge and played at Wimbledon, winning the Gentleman's Singles three years in succession, 1912, 1913 and 1914. There were others including the great Aussies and some Americans. Aaron and I looked forward to possibly playing on Centre Court in the Gentlemen's Doubles.

I spoke with Mirium and apologized for missing her call the night before. I said that I had been out with Frank and decided to stay at his place, since we had gotten in so late. I didn't mention the real reason I hadn't gotten her call. It seemed unnecessary to upset her, when she was trying to be the strong one for her friend. I asked how her friend's husband was doing and she said that the doctors were able to do bypass surgery and that he was mending nicely. He was even joking that he wanted to meet me on the courts when they let him out of the 'prison' as he referred to the hospital. She said she would return the day after tomorrow in time for our next match. After our doubles we all had a few pints, then went to Dom's club for a celebration dinner, courtesy of Dom's brother Alphonse. Susan was there and came right over and sat next to me. She said with her impish grin, "Now that you are a big celebrity are you still talking to me?" She loved all the attention and press we were getting, and she even had a few reporters want to interview her about me and Dom's murder. She was clearly happy to see me.

After midnight we went back to her flat where she seemed even more attentive to me than usual. She didn't want to talk, she just wanted to be held close. She seemed vulnerable tonight and holding her close could only lead to one thing. We had quickly segued into passionate love making. Afterwards, she just wanted to curl up on the couch together and have a quiet drink. I was much too tired to really notice her pensive mood and soon fell asleep with her by my side. At some point during the night, we made our way to the bed. She knew I had to meet Aaron early, but she wouldn't let me out of bed without 'breakfast sex' as she called it. I enjoyed every minute. This was just the preparation I needed for a Center Court doubles match.

That day was the hottest of the week, with the Brits complaining profusely. I loved it, just like Australia. All I needed was to find some ice for my drinks! Frank had an obligation through his business contacts to attend a cricket match that day. Frank's Sports agency, Ace Sports, was the main sponsor, with all donations and proceeds going to charity. It started out as a very informal thing between two rival pubs in the Kensington neighborhood. Aaron and I met up early for a quick practice at Queens to get ready for the doubles match scheduled for the next day. As this was an important day for Frank's business, Aaron and I arrived at the village green at about 11:30. We could see this was a serious cricket match with everyone equipped with proper cricket whites, with official umpires in attendance. Frank obviously wanted me to play for his team. When we arrived, he said, "I never knew an Australian who couldn't play cricket". I dressed in cricket whites that Frank had ready for me, put on the pads, and got ready to go into bat. At that stage of the match, we needed 157 runs to win in two hours of play left. I was still a bit tired from a lack of proper sleep recently, but the anticipation of the game gave me a surge of energy. Frank opened the batting, and we lost his opening partner early and I joined Frank. It felt good to be playing cricket again… I was a bit rusty at first, but then survived the fast bowlers. When they got tired, they brought on the slow bowlers, the spinners and googly specialists. Frank and I clicked and attacked. It turned into a rout. Frank opened his shoulders and hit a towering six over mid-on. We got the runs with time to spare.

Over drinks afterwards, Frank was accused of bringing in a ringer. The other pub players, in jest, suggested no Aussies could play next year… Everyone was very pleased when Aaron donated half his doubles prize money to the charity and Frank matched it. It was a great break from the pressure of the last week and a nice diversion at the right time.

When I got back to the Kensington Palace Hotel, looking forward to a nap, Susan was sitting in the lobby waiting for me. I had discovered, since the funeral, that Susan had a wonderful flame inside her, a flame that needed care to keep burning. Her youth and beauty were hard enough to resist, and her athleticism and energy in making love could be termed borderline addictive, however, she was what I came to know as 'needy'. I wasn't sure if I could do a steady diet of Susan. We went up to my room for a little afternoon delight. Her somewhat forward behavior of showing up unannounced at the hotel was carried over into her bedroom behavior and it wasn't until afterwards that I discovered what was spurring her moods, both last night and this afternoon. We went out for a light supper before she had to be at work, and she told me that she had overheard a conversation at the club about my kidnapping and rescue. It had upset her more than even she realized. I assured her that I was fine and would be safe. All I needed now was a good night's sleep so I could be ready for tomorrow's match. We parted outside of the restaurant as she headed off to the club for work. I watched as she walked away, thinking that she was taking this relationship more seriously than I would have liked, but not sure what to do about it.

15

Second Round Doubles

The next morning was dry with a warm breeze. We could tell it was going to be a hot afternoon. This was one of England's hottest summers on record and the grass courts were getting dry and brown.

We decided to go to practice at Wimbledon so we could get a light massage before the match. I also needed to go to the training room to get my wrist therapy and taping before practice. There was a long history of Aussies qualifying for Wimbledon back as far as the '20's and '30's and I wanted to do as well as I could. Australia had a long tradition of Wimbledon singles champions including Sir Norman Brookes in 1907 and 1914, Jack Crawford in 1933 with his deadly two-handed backhand to the Australian greats of the '50's, '60's and '70's. Likewise, there has been a long dominance of Aussies in men's doubles.

There had been a lot of press about my eventful singles match the week before... For the most part Wimbledon spectators were generally subdued and knowledgeable. They definitely knew their tennis. They also knew I was the Aussie that punched out the murderer. This crowd was in direct contrast to the rowdy, noisy spectators at the US open in New York. However, they were ready for some more excitement when I entered the court. Center Court was to be a challenge, not just because of the crowd noise but it seemed a lot bigger than the outside courts…there was just so much space around it. This was Center Court at Wimbledon, and we were in awe.

The pigeons in the rafters were still there. As we expected, it was very hot and dry with a light breeze coming from the north. When we stepped on the court, we immediately noticed a difference in the footing on the grass and the bounces. Because the weather had been hot and dry the last few days, the court was quicker, the bounce higher and the footing more stable. There were already brown patches around the baselines and service boxes.

As we warmed up, many of the spectators were returning from afternoon tea. There was lots of noise and movement in the stands as they took their seats, and lots of beautiful women. Mirium arrived, as promised, looking elegant and beautiful in a light mauve pantsuit. She took her seat with Frank in our reserved player's box. Aaron and I were determined not to be nervous, and despite being outmatched by the top British pair I felt very proud to be there as a qualifier. I knew my mother and her friends would be watching from Sydney and my student mates and my professors in Eugene and in London would be glued to their televisions. I had to put all of that out of my mind. This afternoon there was only Aaron and I, our opponents, the ball, the net and the grass. Just as I was settling in, to the right frame of mind, my eye caught sight of Susan arriving. This was totally unexpected and quite unnerving. She was alone and sat in the general admission section. I glanced over at Mirium, who was chatting with Frank, and she gave me a small nod and an encouraging smile, before turning her attention back to her conversation. I looked back at Susan, and she looked as excited as I was nervous. I smiled and turned to Aaron, giving a slight tilt of my head in the direction of Susan. He had never met her, but I had described her adequately enough that he immediately recognized her. His look said it all. He obviously thought I was totally out of my mind, having them both there, and he recognized the problem this could cause for my game. He gave me a sharp look directing my attention back to the game. This was not the time to be worrying about women. There was no question though, any thoughts about both Susan and Mirium being there could be a major distraction as we played. He was right, I had to focus and put thoughts of what might happen afterward out of my mind and focus only on our match.

We chose to return serve against the breeze so as Aaron could serve the next game with his swerving skidding lefty serve with the breeze. The umpire called, "Play". In our first game on Center Court, we decided to 'go all out' on our returns. I hit a flat forehand, down the line, on my first return for a winner, and Aaron hit a deft lob over the net man off the second serve return. We felt we could play good grass court tennis, while playing with aggression. We had nothing to lose. We had made it to center court! The crowd erupted when we won the first game. I looked over at Susan and she was beaming and clapping loudly. Mirium and Frank were standing as they applauded our win, both beaming with pride.

Aaron served out the next game to love with several clean aces. Our opponents were clearly shocked. We kept holding serve to take the first set. We were playing well, taking our chances when we could and kept 'going for it'. The next two sets were close, but the Brits just raised their level and played the big points better than we did. The crowd now was eager for a British victory. They played a very professional, methodical fifth set to close out the match,7-5. It was clear by the fifth set, even though we were part time players, and fought hard, that the Brits were better on that day. After the match we nodded to the Royal Box and went straight to the locker room. The crowd gave us all a standing ovation. Frank was waiting for us in the locker room. We had a beer there as we showered and changed.

I asked Frank to find Susan and thank her for coming and tell her I would see her at the club. Frank waited in the player's lounge for us to emerge. When we got there Mirium was drinking a glass of Italian Pinot Grigio and congratulated us on a great match. It was already dusk by then and we decided on an early, leisurely supper. We caught a cab and the driver congratulated me on a great match. We went to her favorite Italian place and the host made a comment about our great showing during the match. It seemed everyone had been watching the match today. Mirium was obviously pleased with the attention I was getting. She seemed genuinely proud to be the woman at my side.

We both ordered 'insalata caprese' and lamb chops, which hands down, had to be the best in London. She ordered a bottle of their finest champagne, a Louis Roederer Cristal to toast our having gotten to Center Court, and how 'spectacularly well' we had played. I felt sad that I would soon have to leave to go back to Oregon to finish my last courses and dissertation. As I was now out of the tournament, I would have to move out of my complimentary suite at the Kensington Palace Hotel. As we toasted life's successes, Mirium asked me to stay with her at Winston Gardens until I had to fly back. I was ecstatic-what a wonderful way to complete the summer. We had a great evening, finally getting to bed after midnight.

Frank had left me a message that Yuri wanted to see us both for lunch at his club. I presumed this was a business meeting for Frank and agreed to go with him. Frank picked me up at the hotel about 11 am. When we arrived at Yuri's club, we weren't quite sure why we were there. We were seated at a spacious round table with very comfortably cushioned bench seating around most of it. Yuri was already seated with a young man to his left. Apparently, this was his young nephew, Michel, and he had wanted to meet us, but I was a bit surprised and confused when he remained at the table after the introductions since we thought this was a business meeting. A waiter brought us drinks and a lunch 'specially selected by Yuri himself'. It consisted of a first course of a cold soup called *okroshka,* consisting of potatoes and cubed bits of ham, I think there was also some cucumber and definitely a strong taste of dill and green onion also. It was very refreshing on a hot day. The traditional 'black' bread was on the table and Yuri bragged that his baker "made the best bread in all of London!" The second course was a dish of a stuffed pasta (I found out later they are called *pelmeni,* stuffed with a pork/beef mixture). They were served with a dollop of sour cream and a sprinkling of dill. A perfect complement to the cold soup. The waiter then brought us each a coffee and placed a tray of small cakes on the table. When we tried to pass the tray to Yuri, he waved them off and patted his stomach, saying he was trying to stay away from the sweets. Conversation during the meal was centered mostly around the current climate, both weather and political. Once the meal was done and the table cleared, Yuri presented Frank with a finalized deed and handed a nice check to me. He thanked us both. He then motioned towards his nephew and explained that he was a promising junior player on the British Junior's team, and he had seen my matches on TV. He found me to be somewhat of an inspiration and hero in his eyes. He wanted to emulate my style on the courts. Yuri asked that when I return next summer if I would coach his nephew in return for a place to stay, a coaching stipend, and all my expenses. This was an offer that I could hardly pass up, made even more appealing by the fact that Yuri was not someone I wanted to disappoint. We agreed to keep in touch, and I took down his nephew's phone number and address. Yuri seemed to be quite content with the outcome of the meeting. It was one of those wonderful encounters where everyone wins and leaves happy. On the way out, Frank said that the nephew was actually a fine young prospect, and I should enjoy coaching him. This deal also gave me even more incentive to come back the next summer.

I was to meet Mirium in my room at the hotel. When I arrived, Investigator O'Neil was seated in the lobby. He offered to buy me a drink and we moved to the hotel bar. I sensed he had something upsetting to tell me, and after he ordered two Tanqueray neats and handed me one, I said, "I assume this isn't a social call." He immediately informed me that the killer had escaped late that morning, en route to the prison the court had remanded him to. It was an obviously professional intervention by some organization that was familiar with the legal process and protocols for transferring prisoners. He suggested that I leave town for a bit, until they could track him down. I told him I was just on my way up to my room to pack and do just that.

I met Mirium in the room and didn't tell her of the conversation with O'Neil. I just, packed my bags in silence. She knew me well enough at this point and sensed something wrong. As she sat on the edge of the bed while I packed, she commented on my apparent preoccupation and silence. I dismissed it as just being totally drained and exhausted by everything that had happened recently and managed to give her a forced smile and a kiss on the forehead. I told her she worries about me too much. We managed to catch the 2:30 pm train for Winston Gardens. We were really looking forward to spending some time together. She suggested that we spend some time visiting her timeshare in St Tropez and visit Cannes and Monte Carlo along the way. I responded with a resounding, "Yes, that would be perfect!". She couldn't have suggested a more perfect idea. This would keep us out of town for a few weeks, and I could keep an eye on her to keep her safe.

16

Back to Winston Gardens

Ever since I first met Mirium she impressed me with her intellect, poise and vision. She was one of a kind. I was privileged to spend time with her. She was an assertive independent woman. She had built a notable diamond company into a fortune after the death of her husband. However, she was subdued about her accomplishments, very generous, and never talked about her recent successes. She had eventually sold the diamond business. That coupled with some timely investments had made her a very wealthy and independent woman. Her beauty to me was in being intelligent, dignified, and quiet. The way her head turned towards the light, the clean line of her jaw, and her deep blue eyes added a discrete look of sincerity. Her silky, smooth skin was doing well with age, it seemed, with little effort. She was indeed a beautiful and wise woman and I felt honored that she wanted to be with me. The combination of physical compatibility and easy companionship were a duo I had never enjoyed before, but I was beginning to realize that we had much more than that together.

I guess, at first it was because she was lonely, had very little family, she chose to spend time with me. We hit it off from the very start and I had to stop her from spoiling me. I could easily get used to it. When we arrived at her house after all the excitement of Wimbledon, I had the feeling of being 'at home'. She had her grass courts perfectly manicured for me to use and she had her cook primed to make all my favorite foods. She clearly wanted me to enjoy myself. She knew I had to go back to finish my dissertation and was very supportive of that objective. She also said she needed a break from her usual routine of country living and of course someone she cared for to spend quality time with. The first evening was such a stark contrast from the environment and events of London that my mind and body felt like I had crashed from a very long adrenalin high. After dinner, Mirium and I sat out on the veranda in some overstuffed wicker chairs, sipping an Armagnac that she gets on her trips to the Riviera. I had never had it before and was instantly won over by its warm cognac like smoothness, that with the first sip, created a feeling of your entire body being aglow. She gets if from a family she has befriended in St. Tropez, who in the French tradition, make it in small batches on their farm. It wasn't long before she was waking me to get me up to bed.

I had Michel, Yuri's nephew, coming in the morning, for a day of drills, play and coaching. I had asked him to come out, rather than wait until next year, so I could get to know him better. In my coaching I was more interested in developing the total person, than just a tennis player. Yuri knew this and would do anything for me. If I were to work with him next year, I wanted to give him a direction to follow in his play and practice this year, so he had a head start on my coaching next year. I had also planned on keeping up with his progress by keeping in touch after I returned to the states.

I was out on Mirium's grass courts practicing with Michel, when an unexpected and unpleasant surprise arrived. Mirium came out to the courts with an envelope addressed to me. It was from Joanne's husband's lawyer, delivered by private courier. I was a bit unnerved that he had been able to track me down out here. If he could, then the killer could. I told Michel to take a break and get some hydration. I opened it and read it out loud to Mirium. She already knew about my time with Joanne in May. Mirium was so good about it, said without hesitation "I will call my lawyer and let him handle it". She was so gracious about it. She knew I was no angel but wanted to keep me stress free and happy to be with her now. She just said, "Stay and finish your practice round and then we'll have lunch." That was it!

Michel and I continued to practice. He was sixteen, good looking and very mature for his age. He was already six feet tall and still growing. He was very attentive and soaked up all my advice like a sponge. We practiced all his strokes and spent most of our time in the morning on his strengths, his forehand and serve. He really needed a better second serve. In the afternoon we spent time on his weaknesses, his backhand and volleys. He needed a lot more time to improve his consistency, and to learn a drop shot and when to use it. After all day of practice, I told Michel he could use one of my suits and spend some time in the indoor pool. It was heated and would be good for his overworked muscles. I recommended some stretches he could do in the pool and after in the spa. We were to meet with Mirium's lawyer at four o'clock over drinks and told Michel we would return by five o'clock for a light snack before taking him to the train home. We knew that his family would expect him to have dinner with them upon his return and did not want to interfere with that.

Mirium's lawyer met us promptly at four o'clock. Mirium was one of his most valued clients. He said this happens in a lot of divorce proceedings to help reduce alimony. He said he could take care of everything and not to give it a second thought. When we got back to the house, we found a cheese and pastry sampler and some iced tea made with fruits and berries waiting for us. Michel was particularly pleased with the tea, as it was similar to what he would get for lunch at home. I took him back to his train for London in Mirium's Jaguar as twilight descended like a curtain closing. I was beginning to feel relaxed and 'normal' once again.

I awoke to another perfect late summer day-a bit warmer than usual. On the south facing terrace of the house, I could see the bright colors of Mirium's rose garden and her two finely manicured lawn tennis courts, and the green rolling hills in the background. The birds were chattering, and all was good in my world.

One of the highlights of Winson Gardens was that we could ride Mirium's horses. My mount was "not used to being ridden" according to Mirium, was very high spirited at first, and almost threw me a few times. Mirium, an excellent horsewoman, sat very erect in the saddle. She said she had "missed her daily rides in the countryside" and was glad for my company. I had ridden a little before in the outback on rough stock horses but was much out of practice. Gradually as we rode, my horse calmed down and made me look like an expert... We rode for several hours, that day, in brilliant sunshine, galloping a bit, over branches, gorse, bracken, and over ditches. I found myself captivated by Mirium, with her slim, erect figure, her control over her mount, her wispy, disordered hair and now flushed cheeks. We stopped at the edge of a meadow where the shade allowed the grass to stay green and tall. It was as if we were the only two people on earth. There was a brook where the horses were able to get water. We sat in the grass, and as I looked around innocently, I reached over and began to unbutton her blouse. She cleared her throat and I turned to look at her with a sheepish grin. We lay in the grass and made love. Now I know why women love to ride.

Mirium and I spent the next few days touring the countryside, visiting with some of her friends and seeing the sights. We spend a night on the coast at a bed and breakfast, then headed inland to stay with some friends for a couple of days. It worried me that the courier found me and I tried to keep us away from the house as much as possible without raising any alarms. Playing the part of a curious tourist provided the excuse to stay on the move. O'Neil had suggested that the killer might lay low for a bit or may even leave the country. There was no way to tell or guess what he might do, but I was the one person who could ID him as being at the scene of Dom's murder. I felt a need to keep moving. Yuri knew of our plans to head to the Riviera, and I trusted that he would not divulge that information.

17

Susan

On the weekend I had a commitment with Frank to do some promotional exhibitions and clinics for Slazenger. We were to do clinics for kids at a public facility in East London. This was part of the LTA's program to 'grow the game'. Most of the kids were from recent immigrant and black neighborhoods. The press would be there, which was not a good thing for me but it would be good for Frank's business. I felt badly after not seeing Susan after the doubles match, so I called her at the club. We agreed to meet that night.

I caught an early train back to the city, leaving Mirium at her estate at Winston Gardens. She knew about the promotional commitments that Frank and I had in London. She expected me back on Monday and would meet me at the station on my return. We were both looking forward to our time together on the Riviera.

Frank and I conducted our clinics with the help of some volunteers. We had a great afternoon and lots of fun. Frank supplied enough rackets and balls for all the kids and the BBC had a great time taking video for the night's news. The clinic focused on helping everyone have maximum participation and for all to enjoy themselves. Everyone got a new racket to take home, courtesy of Slazenger. Yuri Grosegann's nephew, Michel, showed up first thing at noon to help out, which turned out to be a lifesaver, considering the number of kids that showed up for the clinic. His enthusiasm for the game was genuine and I think the kids were finding it contagious. He was a natural teacher and great at building up self-esteem and confidence. I could tell he was already practicing the skills that we had gone over during his visit. His driver never seemed to be far, as if he were there as a bodyguard as well. But was it for Michel or for me? Even though the killer's escape was kept under wraps, there was no doubt in my mind that Yuri knew about it.

I arrived at Susan's flat, just after midnight… I still had a key. I let myself in and instantly smelled her perfume. She had prepared a cozy light supper. She had some palatable Pinot Grigio in her fridge, canapes, snacks and salads prepared. When she arrived after work at midnight, she was very pleased to see me. She said she enjoyed watching me play and asked if I would possibly teach her how to play. She had the day off the next day, Sunday, and I said I would give her, her first tennis lesson tomorrow.

Hearing this, she went straight to her overfilled closet and dug out her tennis racket, an older beat-up model with a broken string. She was excited to learn and to spend some time with me. After supper I showed her about stance, swing and grip. She liked the personal touch and was excited to learn.

Her flat was a comfortable size, just one bedroom off of the living room/dining room combination. The kitchen was small but well laid out. She kept the apartment neat and clean, and she said it was all she needed. Dom got it for her before he died, and his brother was paying the rent as long as she worked as a waitress/hostess at the club. We had a good long talk that night about her life so far. She had a pretty basic high school education and some training in the hotel restaurant business. She really wanted to be an actress though. She was very beautiful, carried herself with confidence, but lacked any experience. She said she really enjoyed my company, moved closer, looked into my eyes and caressed my cheek tenderly. I still felt she was a bit young and immature for me, but I really liked her company, and it was hard to resist the great sex.

I was, in fact trying out Frank's secrets of dealing with women and concentrated on just listening. This paid off. She enjoyed this and this seemed to be good therapy for both of us. We agreed that I should stay the night and give her a tennis lesson in the morning. It was late and it started to thunder. She took my hand in both of hers and gave me a girlish smile, saying, "the thunder scares me. Can we hide under the covers?" as she pulled me up out of the chair and led me into the bedroom. pushed me down and kissed me all over. The thunder and lightning outside just seemed to intensify her passion. As we made love, it seemed as if her body was in tune to the rhythm of the storm. We woke to a hazy sunrise and a more subdued, but very satisfying copulation.

We had a late breakfast of cereal and warmed croissants. We walked in her neighborhood to a tennis court in a local park, where I gave her the tennis lesson as promised. Her athleticism gave her a strong advantage, along with the flexibility and quick reflexes we all enjoy in our younger years. Add to that the fact that she was an attentive student and quick learner and I found myself anticipating future practice matches with her, with the inevitable post-match bedroom activities…or maybe locker room. I needed to focus. She moved well around the court and learned quickly. The most important thing she had to learn was how to watch the ball-especially on ground strokes when she needed to watch the bounce, and on volleys how to let the ball hit the racket without swinging too much. Tennis is a game of steps and throws—I had her throw the ball overhand as with a throw in preparation for serving. Tennis is also a game of projecting and receiving. I emphasized her finding her own natural rhythm, stroking the ball, tracking its pathway and finding how to control it. She seemed to genuinely enjoy her lesson. As we were leaving, I noticed a car that had been parked across the street the entire time we were there pull from the curb. If I didn't know better, I would say that Yuri was providing me with a certain amount of protection. The killer was still at large.

We went to a movie and went out to a local Indian restaurant for dinner. The Indian food in London at that time was the best, always simple, fresh ingredients, with as much or as little spices as you might like. We had a great day and evening.

The next morning, I had a cab waiting for me to take me to the station. As I was leaving her place, we said our goodbyes. She knew I was going away for several weeks to the Riviera, thinking I had tennis commitments there. Then I had to go back to the states. We said goodbyes at her front door...she avoided my eyes...avoiding my lips like she was stepping over a hole in the ground... She just squeezed my hands and hugged me. A single tear fell to her cheek. Susan was beautiful even when she was crying. I looked forward to seeing her again when I returned next year, just to see her eyes light up.

It was grey and misting out now as I made my way to the station. The heat of the last week had dissipated. I wondered if Agassi would get used to the grass courts enough to win Wimbledon. I took a nap on the train as I hadn't had much sleep. Mirium was waiting for me at the station and had me drive her new Jaguar home. It was good to see her.

We left for Cannes the next day. Yuri sent his private jet to pick us up at the nearby airport. Mirium loved it!

18

Cannes

We landed at the Cannes-Mandelieu Airport, at the west end of Cannes in mid-afternoon to bright sunshine, a warm breeze and salt air. Only a short two-hour non-stop flight from England, yet a stark contrast to the overcast, rainy and smog filled air of London. Mirium had arranged for a car, and a Mercedes C Class sat waiting for us. She had suggested that we stay a couple of nights in Cannes. Cannes, of course, is famous for their film festival in June. Finding a room anywhere remotely near here would have been impossible had we arrived during that week, however, we were here near the end of the tourist season. Crowds were not a problem and the travelers who visited the area this time of year simply blended into the overall charm and character of the town. Mirium was keen to show me the sights of Cannes and Monte Carlo before we drove down the coast to her place in St. Tropez. She had us booked into the historic and opulent Martinez Hotel for two nights. The airport was only a few minutes from the hotel by highway, but she insisted on taking the more scenic route along the beach. The drive began in a more industrial area, with the beach on our right, but soon transformed into a narrow, tree-lined boulevard, with the beach and marinas on our right and majestic old buildings on our left. Two historic hotels, the Martinez and the Carlton were next door to each other, right on the water, with their own private beach and easy access for guests to both hotels. As we drove up to the valet at the front entrance in the Mercedes, I had the distinct feeling of being somewhat outclassed by the other cars at the curb. Our ride looked very modest in the company of Bentley's, Lamborghini's and Rolls.

As they unloaded our bags, we walked through the front doors to a room that can be described as nothing less than magnificent. We felt we were stepping back in time. The old-world charm maintained with high, ornately embellished ceilings supported by large, Corinthian columns with soft Persian rugs cushioning the path over the Italian marble floors. Artistically crafted, arabesque wall features added to the overall beauty everywhere you looked. Palms scattered throughout softened the entire look and added to the welcoming ambiance.

We were escorted up to our room, a suite on the sixth floor with magnificent views of the Mediterranean, completely remodeled but again preserving the grand tradition of the great hotels of Europe of a century ago.

The double doors were opened for us to enter and we walked into a world surrounded by luxury, from the plush carpet beneath our feet to the elaborately coffered ceilings. The furnishings were reminiscent of renaissance royalty with a breathtaking view of the harbor. We opened the windows and balcony doors to allow some of the fresh Mediterranean air indoors and decided to take advantage of the view. We rang up room service for a bottle of some fine French champagne. I felt a warm gentle breeze stroking my hair as I stood on the balcony sipping my champagne and letting my fingers run along the intricately crafted wrought iron railing. The salt air enveloped me with thoughts of a late-night walk along the beach below. The aromas wafting up from the cafe's and bistro's were teasing my senses with promises of culinary delights to come.

Mirium had all the qualities I admired. She was mature, beautiful, buoyant, and independent. Every day was a new experience for me. She had been coming to the French Riviera at least once a year for many years and she enjoyed watching me share this experience with her. I felt privileged to be with her. Right from the start we both reveled in the French cuisine. What would appear a small hole-in-the-wall café, with perhaps ten tables, would produce their specialties which were out of this world. The menu of three or four dishes would be on a blackboard and change each night, depending on what fish, produce and meats were available locally that day. At Cafe Isis, about a block from our hotel, down a side lane, frequented only by locals, I experienced morels for the first time, with roasted rabbit—-magnifico!

The excitement of the last weeks at Wimbledon, the travel, and the warm sunshine, overtook us and before we knew it, we had sipped our way through a full bottle of champagne before five o'clock. At that point we just flopped on the bed, giddy, making love as if it were a silly game. After becoming more seriously involved in our activity, we finally fell asleep in each other's arms for a much-needed nap.

When we stirred after our nap, we were ravenously hungry. We took a short walk along the Ocean Boulevard, then enjoyed a drink at the lobby bar, which was elaborately decorated to take you back to 1925 the moment you walked in. We went back upstairs, showered together and dressed for dinner. She said both the Martinez and the Carlton had magnificent dining. We looked at the menu in our room then went downstairs. She ordered for me, choosing duck, and the fish of the day for her. It was all so good we shared plates and devoured every morsel.

The next day we woke early. While we were getting ready to head across the road to the hotel's private beach, we tuned in to the news. The commentator immediately caught our attention with the name Sean McNeece. With all of the unrest in London, it was a name that came up in the news frequently and his recent capture made international headlines. They were reporting that the notorious Irish bomber and kidnapper had escaped while being transferred, in custody, to Old Bailey Jail to await trial. Two policemen were killed. There was a nationwide and international manhunt underway. I was not concerned about his escape, as I had nothing to do with his capture. As the victim, I was more of an innocent bystander during the raid. I had still failed to mention that whole ordeal to Mirium and I had also not told her of the escape of the killer. It all seemed like a million miles away. I did, unfortunately, show my cards by making a comment on the escape. "Scotland Yard is having a bad time of it. Two escapes in two weeks! You'd think after the first one, they would have changed their protocol." I was feeling so far away from all of that unpleasantness that the comment came out before I realized what I was saying. I'm not particularly good at hiding the truth. I almost bit my tongue, hoping she wouldn't pick up on my comment, but Mirium pays too much attention to details to have let that slide.

"What do you mean, two escapes? I don't remember hearing about any others." She could read my expression too well for me to make any attempt at hiding things from her at this point. It seemed like a good time to come clean. I was going to start with a very weak "I've been meaning to tell you" but that even sounded lame to me. I simply said, "Do you remember when I was a bit late getting to the hotel when we were leaving and wasn't talking much?" "Yes?" she said in a very suspicious and questioning voice. I guided her over to the chair and had her sit down. Her expression was transitioning from curious to concerned. "When I got back to the hotel, Inspector O'Neil was waiting for me in the lobby." I then proceeded to relate our conversation about the killer being on the loose. Her face had gone from the healthy glow she had developed on our vacation to a shade of white, as the blood drained from her cheeks. She sat still and processed this bit of information, seemingly not sure whether she should be angry or fearful. I stood there afraid to breath, while the jury was still out on her reaction, then I took in a long breath and said, "That's not all."

True to human nature, she immediately assumed the worst, though for the life of me I couldn't imagine anything she could dream up being worse that what I just told her. This normally cool, calm and collected woman before me looked like she was on the verge of hysterics. A thought popped into my head and I blurted out "It's not another woman!" Her shoulders instantly relaxed and she caught her breath and started to breath normally. She had regained her composure and simply said, "What else?".

I related the entire story from the time I left her at the station, until we met again, obviously omitting the time spent with Susan.

She sat in silence and listened as I shared every moment and thought during the ordeal. At this point, I didn't want to leave anything out. I hadn't realized how badly I had wanted to share this with her, until I started the story. I finished and waited for her response. She stood up and walked across the room without uttering a word. It seemed like an eternity before she said anything, but she was an intelligent woman who knew better than to speak before thinking. At that moment, I just wished that I knew what was going on in her mind.

She finally turned towards me and said, "I'm hurt that you didn't tell me all of this sooner." I responded that, "there is no excuse, except that I didn't want to upset you or worry you. Our time together was so perfect, I didn't want to ruin it. I really wanted to tell you, to tell you everything." I added, "And I am so sorry for not trusting in your strength as a woman to be able to cope with all of this." I'm not sure, but I think the last statement was the tipping point on the scale in my favor. She quietly walked over to me while keeping her eyes locked on mine. I think I was actually bracing for a slap across the face. Instead, she reached out to embrace me around the waist and lowered her head to nuzzle her face against my neck. I drew her in closer to me and we stood in silence for a moment or two. She drew back from me and said if we were to have time at the beach, we should head on down.

It was beautifully warm. The sun was still low enough in the sky that we weren't baked by its rays and the cheerful umbrellas helped to shade our thickly cushioned chaise lounges. We enjoyed the service of cool mimosas, as we worked up to entering the very cool Mediterranean water. The sand here at Cannes was not sand as I was used to in Australia. It was more like small pebbles, common in this part of the Mediterranean, but the cool water was clean and refreshing. As we looked out to the sea, the sun was glinting off the polished decks and masts of the sailing yachts and we could see a luxury motor yacht leaving its berth and heading out to parts unknown.

We swam out to the pontoon off the beach, sat in the sun and enjoyed the scene. We had some discussion about the events I had told her about this morning and whether or not I felt safe down here. I assured her that I never felt safer, or happier, in my entire life. As she rose to dive into the water again, she looked exquisite in her dark blue one-piece bathing suit. Even the back of her was impressive with her straight back, square shoulders and gorgeous long legs. We swam back to the beach—she was a strong swimmer. As I walked up the beach, I couldn't help but reflect on how lucky I was to be here in Cannes with this beautiful, strong and understanding woman. A far cry from my modest apartment, schoolgirl type students and muggy summer weather of Oregon.

After our swim we went back up to our suite and decided to take the short drive along the coast to famed Monte Carlo. Monte Carlo is in Monaco, a Royal municipality within France. It is the home of many celebrities, and since Boris Becker moved there it has become a tax haven for many of the top tennis players. Residents of Monaco pay little or no taxes so many movie stars and professional athletes maintain a residence here for at least a part of the year. Consequently, it has all the quality amenities attractive to the rich and famous including spectacular exclusive shopping, The Beach Club, the Casino and the Monte Carlo Tennis Club of which Prince Rainier is a patron and avid tennis player. Every year in April the prince hosts the Monte Carlo Open on the red clay courts overlooking the spectacular view of the Mediterranean. We walked around the boutiques and had a quiet drink on the verandah overlooking the tennis courts.

From there we decided to take a drive up the mountain above Monte Carlo where we got a spectacular view of the Casino and the Royal Palace. It was a beautiful sunny day, with the sun starting to drop in the west. We soon found one of Mirium's favorite restaurants, high above the coast. The specialty was Chateaubriand cooked as only the French can do-rare and crusty on the outside, with the vegetables roasted to perfection. We had frog's legs and oysters to start and exquisite pastries and local cheeses to finish. We drove back down the treacherous mountain road—the same road where Grace Kelly, famous actress and Princess of Monaco was killed, driving too fast. We could see why? It was a dangerous, steep, winding two miles, with certain death if you got out of control over the side. On the way back we drove by the famous hundred-year-old Casino, again, with the Bentleys, Porsches, Maseratis and Rolls Royces parked out-side. We stayed on the coast road for the beginning of the trip to enjoy the sunset as we drove. When going through Nice to get on the highway, Mirium made a comment about us spending some time there next year, to enjoy the Cote d'Azur observatory, and the Marc Chagall and Matisse museums. We were glad to be back at our hotel and Mirium agreed we should head down the coast the next morn-ing after a swim, where we had a more tranquil stay arranged at her condo in St. Tropez.

19

St. Tropez

After all the excitement and hustle and bustle of Cannes and Monte Carlo Mirium and I were ready for some quiet time. St. Tropez is about ninety minutes down the coast road from Cannes. As we drove south it became less populated with few if any tourists. It was around lunch time when we reached the town, with its fishing boats, lots of colorful awnings and umbrellas around the cafes and bistros along the water. We stepped out of the car at her favorite lunch spot and immediately took in the relaxed, laid back atmosphere of the town. This was such a contrast to the wealth and opulence around the Carlton and Martinez.

When we finally arrived at the condo she had booked for the week, it was late afternoon. The caretakers, a young Italian couple, had already stocked the kitchen with essentials including crisp, flaky croissants and pastries for us to have for breakfast the next day. We took a walk along the beach. There was a stiff, warm breeze off the water. Mirium's carefully pulled back hair was just disturbed enough by the breeze to frame her face with soft wisps of brown, with highlights of gold from the reflection of the streetlamps. Peeking in at a few of the waterside cafes, we delighted in the smells and sounds of simple uncluttered French provincial food. We picked out several we must try during the next few nights. We decided we would try a different place every night. They were all outstanding, with the local, fresh, mouthwatering seafood, local lamb and fine Bordeaux wines. We planned to spend our days swimming every morning, wandering the unhurried shops, soaking up the light sea breezes and enjoying the local foods and spirits. Much of our afternoons were spent in ideal chit chat with locals, sitting around in the outdoor cafés, over expresso or wine, or both. The fresh assortments of *des pâtisseries* seemed endless. I was wondering how I was going to be able to return to my life before this summer. This was really living the dream.

The last night we wanted to use up every minute we could enjoying the sights, sea air and sounds of St. Tropez, so we went to one of our favorite restaurants, La Poisson du Maison, that had outdoor seating overlooking the bay, on a patio that surrounded each table with bushes smothered in roses, gardenias, jasmine, honeysuckle and countless other flowering shrubs and trees. Each setting was like being in your own personal garden, away from anyone else. As we were being led through the interior dining room, to the veranda, I came to an abrupt halt. I couldn't believe my ears, but when I looked around, sure enough, that unmistakable accent was not my imagination this time. I peered out from behind a large wood column at a table tucked back in the corner. The man at the table was wearing a wig, dark glasses and a Panama hat, but there was no mistaking. It was Sean McNeece in the flesh. He was sitting at a table with four chairs, two of which were occupied with two cheap looking women. There was a glass in front of the fourth as if someone had been sitting there. The women looked like they had been up all night. One of the women had kicked off her shoes and had drawn up one leg onto her chair under her bottom, exposing her bare foot, upper thigh and black lace panties. She had one arm draped over McNeece's shoulder and he was contentedly stroking her breasts while the women appeared to be happily involved in conversation. I was about to continue to our table and tell Mirium of my find, when the fourth person stepped into my view. I put my hand up to my mouth to stifle a loud gasp. There was no mistaking the tall dark figure. He said something to McNeece that made them both laugh as he sat down with his back to me. Then I heard him say that if he had to be on the run, this wasn't a bad place to be. Another couple were making their way out to the veranda and I moved in next to them to block the view from the corner table as I hurried toward Mirium. She asked "Where did you disappear to? I was worried!" I quickly filled her in on who our fellow patrons were, and she went pale. "They didn't see me. I'm sure!" I flagged down the Maître d', gave him a brief explanation, pointing out the fugitive's table and asked him to call the police. Ten minutes later, we noticed several cars pulling up in front of the restaurant and two lines of armed police at a discreet distance along the beach, on either side of the building. Four officers came through the door, two staying at the doorway. When McNeece saw the officers approaching, he knocked one of the girls on the floor and made a run for the back of the building. The killer didn't even bother to turn around and look, just followed his lead. The "Halt!" by the police had no effect, but they apparently preferred not to discharge a weapon in a public place. Due to the foliage and plants around the guests on the patio, the view of the fleeing fugitives and ensuing police chase was heard but not visible, however, the sound of four gunshots piercing the evening air was unquestionable. The chatter at the tables had become somewhat of a din as everyone was asking the staff what had happened. They assured everyone that even though they didn't have the details, everything was under control and there was no danger to any of the patrons. A few moments later the Maître d' came over to our table and said my presence was requested outside by the Detective in charge. Mirium grasped my hand as if afraid this was a ruse and I patted it reassuringly. I met the detective in the street as some of the other officers were carrying two body bags through the alley between the buildings. The fugitives saw the police in front of them and fired off one shot each before the police they didn't notice behind them shot them in the back. Both were killed instantly. The two shots the fugitives got off grazed one officer on the leg and hit another in the shoulder. He wanted to thank me for taking the initiative of reporting their location. I explained to him that one of them had killed a friend of mine and the other had kidnapped me. I had no love for these two men and no remorse about how this ended.

I returned to our table and my dear Miriam and filled her in. We both sat in silence for a moment as the realization that there was no more danger for us, sunk in. We slowly began to smile at one another, and I lifted my glass in a toast. "Here's to no more fear and no more secrets!" We sat there drinking wine and laughing about anything and everything until they finally asked us to leave so they could close and go home. The next morning, we packed up the car and headed back to Cannes, taking the coast road all the way, enjoying every last moment along the sea. We vowed to return the next year. We got back to the airport just in time for our return flight and before we knew it, we had landed in London and were on the train heading back to Winston Gardens. We were picked up at the station by the butler. It had started to rain by the time we got in the car.

20

Time to Leave

I awoke one last time to the sounds of chattering wrens in the garden outside our window. I rolled over and kissed Mirium on the forehead. It was time for me to leave. She rolled over and hugged me and kissed my hands. The soft kisses aroused me. She giggled as she felt the reaction and took it as in invitation to continue with more kisses on my neck and soft breathing in my ear. Her breasts were against my chest and I suddenly wanted her more than I ever had. But I also wanted this to last forever. It took all of my will to make slow and powerful love to her, bringing her close to orgasm, then keeping her their as long as I could bare it. When we finally climaxed together it was as if the entire world had exploded around us. We collapsed in the bed and lay there until there was a knock on the door and breakfast was brought in.

After we ate, I started packing my bag. She said I should leave my 'English clothes' in her closet. I left my two Harris tweed sports jackets, a Burberry's suit, my French silk pajamas and my dinner tuxedo. I would not be needing them that year at school. Somehow, a part of me was glad to be getting on with my life. The underworld undertones I had been entangled with this trip were, on one side, exciting and provocative, but on the other were well outside of my comfort zone. I was looking forward to 'normal'. I would, however, definitely miss Mirium.

As I finished packing and said, "I guess that's everything." Mirium's expression darkened, as though a cloud had passed over, casting a dark shadow on her face. She immediately appeared distraught and squeezed my hand. "I have a lot of work and organizing of my research to do before I arrange to meet with my doctoral advisor by mid-September, and if I'm to graduate in May, I need to get started actually writing my dissertation. I had not gotten as much research completed over the summer as I had hoped." I added with a smile, "Things kept coming up."

I had booked my Qantas flight back to the states, LAX, then from Los Angeles to Eugene, Oregon. I was not pleased to be leaving. I will miss the excitement and especially my beautiful, wise and tranquil Mirium. I will miss her greatly.

I called Uri to thank him for his generosity. He said how much Michel had enjoyed my coaching. He said they both looked forward to seeing me next summer. Mirium wished me good luck with my studies and said she was already making plans for next year. It was a tearful farewell when I left Mirium.

After all the press and notoriety, I had an invitation to visit Oxford before my departure. Frank met my train and drove me there. They offered me a post-doctoral fellowship for the next year—another good chance to remain in London longer, we had a quick farewell lunch at the airport, and he saw me to my gate. Frank promised to come and visit me at Christmas and to plan a celebration for me as Dr Hardigan in May. What an unbelievable summer this was. I looked forward to next year.

As I settled in for the long flight, I opened a book and found a note I had written to myself long ago as a bookmark. It was a belief of the aboriginals: "*The people we love live on inside us*". I now understood that.

The End

About the Author

D r. David J Staniford has been a tennis professional for more than forty years. A native of Sydney, Australia, he began his teaching career in the Australian outback. Coached by the legendary Australian Davis Cup coach, Harry Hopman, David was a former number one player at the University of Oregon. An outstanding Australian junior tennis player he studied at Sydney Teacher's College and the University of New South Wales. He went on to become an expert in movement analysis, studying at University of Oregon, and the University of London. He has taught and coached players at the University of Oregon, Illinois State University, Brock University in Ontario, Canada, Newberry College, and Marquette University.

His course, 'A Movement Approach to Sports Skills' has been taught in many countries. He teaches and consults with players, teams and coaches on movement and skills technique. He continues to conduct tennis clinics and camps around the world. Several of his players have played Davis Cup for their countries. His books include Natural Movement for Children; Kendall Hunt, and Natural Tennis, second Edition; Stipes with John Boaz. Good Strokes for Senior Folks; The New You Publishing. He continues to write articles for professional magazines. Presently he is the Tennis Professional at Savannah Lakes Village (SLV), a master-planned, community in McCormick, South Carolina, where he has inspired league play for the residents and taken teams to both state and national competitions. David has made tennis his life, and in return it has afforded him many once-in-a-lifetime experiences.

CPSIA information can be obtained
at www.ICGtesting.com
Printed in the USA
JSHW020224220322
24103JS00001B/100